the cabal

I dedicate this book to my parents Curtis and Nadine, who taught me the value of education, faith, and hard work. It's through their lessons I learned to be the change I want to see in this world; my wife Laneishia for her unending love and support. You bring color to my black and white world; and most importantly my daughter Vanessa the most precious thing in my life. These are the people that make me all that I am. These people are my purpose.

This work is also a dedication to my friends and supporters that have heavily influenced it's tone and subject matter. You encouraged me to push towards the finish line. This book feels like it represents a transformative chapter in my life and I'm privileged to share my journey. Special thank you to the following: Kippy "Ayokipp" Warren, Prescott Aiken, Mikal McClurken, Nikki Stephens, Tyree "Hotboi Ty" Robinson, Jasmin Stephanie Reichertz, Laura "Aulelei" Mouton, Regine Abel, Malcolm "Muddy1k" Carter, Melven Eatman, Crystyle Stockdale, Cedric Bellamy, Shannon Jenkins, Marcus Flores, Trell Brennan, Javarious White, Terrence "Doc" Williams and Kendrell Marshall

AND MY TEAM AT

THE

CABAL

THE CEZAR AND BRUTUS ALLIANCE LOUNGE

Official Playlist

Hip-Hop and R&B Classics inspired by the story and its characters.
Selected by author Curtis Maxwell II

APPLE MUSIC

SPOTIFY

one
midnight maurader

JANUARY IS the coldest month of the year. The holidays are over for those that can afford the luxury of things like that. The excitement of a new year isn't felt on the 300 Block of Lincoln Way. The first of January is a time of anxiety, but then again, so is the 15th. It's the same every month. You can see the snowfall from the 'burbs and sing "White Christmas" and ski and ice skate and whatever else white people do. Doesn't know any. Well, that's not true, really. There's J.D. he's probably the only white guy's ever seen in the neighborhood. It's hard to really describe "JD" as a guy at all. Fiends that far gone are hardly human. They're animals, plain and simple. They're wild eyed desperate, and dangerous, but that can be used. Anybody can be used. At least that's the last thing's boy Black told him. Black understood that better than anyone, but he's dead now, and that's the cost of that kind of understanding: Street Smarts. If an early grave is the price of street smarts, had done his best to stay as ignorant as possible lately at least, but now ... Now there's just the cold.

The people in the burbs watch the snow fall, but they don't see it land in the street, turn grey and grimy and freeze into ice. Ice in the street can be as lethal as any gun. People are no different. If you stay in the street long enough, you become grimy and cold. Life in the city is never-ending winter. No matter how long you try to avoid the cold,

1

eventually, it will find you and freeze you from the inside out. For Lincoln-Way, the first sign of winter began with a single snowflake. For, it began with a single phone call.

The only thing on Rico's mind, other than the cold, was the call. The call was the only thing in the world that could have gotten him outside at 6am in the dead of winter. Rico thought about this as he crunched through the ice in his black Nike ACG boots. Water was starting to seep in where the stitching had separated from the sole but fuck it. What could you expect when you buy $100 Nike Boots out front of the barbershop for $30? You get out of it what you put into it. Rico knew that rule applied to everything in life. That was his understanding. It's what drove him to pursue that upcoming management position at Food Shark. He had worked there since he was 14 to help put food on the table for his mother and sister. Once his mother died leaving them the house, he continued grinding his way to the top to keep food in the fridge and, of course, $30 knockoffs on his feet. He put everything into his work because Management was the one thing he knew he could do well. He managed his money, his time, the affairs of his sister, and his duties as assistant manager at Food Shark. It was second nature to him after years of managing to be the man of the house his whole life. He managed without a father ...

The thought of it brought him back to the phone call. It was maybe an hour ago. The familiar sound of his prepaid plastic phone woke him from a dreamless sleep. He answered: "Hello?" barely conscious.

"Is this Lil Rico?" was the reply. He hadn't been called "Lil" Rico in years. His mother's friends used to call him that, but the voice on the other end of the line didn't sound like someone he knew or a friend for that matter.

"Who is this?" he demanded. The response came as quickly and unexpectedly as the phone call itself.

"Listen, we don't have time for long conversations and shit. I'm your ... 'Uncle,' and your father was recently killed. Before you tell me you don't have one, you should know that I knew your mother Linda very well back in the day."

The sound of his mother's name hit him like a fist in the dark. Everybody knew Gladys, but her middle name was known only to Rico

2

and his sister. Hearing it come from the raspy voice on the phone was not only unexpected, but it was also almost disrespectful.

"Look, I don't know who you are or what the fuck you want, but you don't' know shit about me or my—"

"Like I said, we don't have time for this. Your father is dead, and we have a lot of ... business to discuss. You need to know things and there are people you need to meet. Your father left you an inheritance ... The type that doesn't require a will. You wanna know more about it all, then be at the Quick Trip outside of Lincoln Way by 6:30. I'll pick you up and give you what's rightfully yours. Oh, and don't worry about heading into Food Shark at 7. Just get to the QT like your life depends on it because it does. Oh yeah, you might wanna move quick cause the snow gonna soak into those fake ass boots before you know it."

And then he hung up. There wasn't a lot of time to think. The clock was ticking, and Rico had to know more about what was going on. The number on the phone was unknown, and the voice on the other end was cold and unfamiliar. Rico was ready in 15 minutes. A quick splash of soapy water and a brush-up was all he needed before he threw on some jeans, a thermal, and a black hooded letterman-styled winter coat. Once dressed, he grabbed a cup of water and a cold Poptart, eating it quickly as he threw on a black Carolina Panthers skullcap. Maybe he should tell his sister, he thought, but when he glanced in her room, he saw it was empty, again. Where the fuck did she always go? If she was running the street hoeing or fiend-out, he would have known by now because the streets talk. He realized that it wasn't the time to contemplate his sister's location at this hour. He had a crucial decision to make: Should he bring Silver?

Silver was a Bersa .380; he got as a gift from Black when his mother died.

It was black and grey and had six bullets. "Hollow Points" Black had called them. The pistol held eight bullets, but Rico had fired one to test the weapon and later one to scare a crack fiend trying to break into his house. Guns were for drug dealers and gangsters. He'd had some experiences in dealing with both. Ironically, however, he kept one to protect his family from those same dealers and gangsters. Rico decided to take the gun because one thing, one part of the conversation stuck in his mind "your father was recently killed."

What did that mean? Who was his father that someone would want to kill him? He couldn't have been legit because he didn't have a will. A dope fiend wouldn't have an inheritance to leave. A pimp would have had a woman make the call. Rico knew the faces of the hustlers, the dope boys of the neighborhood. Who didn't? Who was his father? More importantly to Rico: If he left an inheritance, that meant he *knew* he had a son. The pain of being fatherless was one that Rico learned to bury a long time ago, but the knowledge that he had been deliberately left fatherless reawakened and intensified it.

This intensity urged him to meet this mysterious caller and demand answers more than anything else. He didn't give a damn about an inheritance. He didn't want to know what his father left him. He wanted to know *why* his father left him. These thoughts consumed his focus until they were interrupted by another phone call.

"I'm fucking coming, so stop playing games." Was his greeting.

"Um ... hi Rico," was the response. It was Mr. Weston, his boss.

"Rico, due to some unfortunate circumstances I've been... Rico, we have to let you go."

The news almost made him smash his phone into 100 pieces. How would he pay the bills? How would he eat? He worked so hard. Why was he being fired? Finally, why did Mr. Weston call him at 5:30 AM? He never calls this early.

"Don't worry about coming in today. Your final check will be deposited later today and will include three months advance pay. Your paystub'll be mailed to your home. I'm sure you have things to do, so I'll make this brief; you're smart, hard-working, and born to lead. Never forget... to trust your gut. Good luck Rico."

"But Mr. Weston ... " He started to reply, but the line was dead, along with any hope of being a store manager. Mr. Weston almost sounded robotic or nervous. Excited? Rico figured he would go to Food Shark later and get his job back; at least they'd make him a stock boy, right? With that decided, there was nothing to stop him from his meeting. So, he headed to the door and stepped out into the cold.

Now, with his foot freezing, Rico was on his way to meet his caller.

Walking through his neighborhood was like walking through the world's most fucked up jewelry store. Be careful what you do because you're always being watched, and even the slightest mistake can cost you more than you ever thought. Black had paid that price, and it sounded like Rico's father had too.

Father.

Rico wasn't even sure he believed the caller was telling the truth about that. What he was sure of, however, was that the caller knew his mother and, more importantly, was watching him. He pointed out Rico's boots to prove that he had eyes on Rico. Rico got the message.

Rico knew the caller knew his number, where he worked, what he wore, and his mother. Hell, maybe he did know his father. The more Rico thought about it, the more dangerous the caller seemed. A six-shot .380 wasn't nearly enough to make Rico feel comfortable dealing with this guy, but it would have to do.

"Ricky Rick-Ricky Ricky-Ricky Rico sua-ve"'

A vocal DJ scratching sound? The sound broke his concentration as he looked to see it was old June. The crackhead/wino. He used to go by "June Bug" before his addictions turned ugly.

"Sup June," Rico said nonchalantly as he kept walking

"Aye Rico Aye-Aye ha-ha! where are you going?" June was walking beside him now.

"To the store really quick."

"OK, OK, OK, I'm picking up what chu' putting down," June said in a pseudo-accepting tone. "Hold up real quick, man, let me show you my move. Shiiiit, I used to kill'em with this one." June said as he attempted some awkward dance moves. "Ka-Ci and JoJo couldn't tell me shit!"

"Sorry, June, but I am busy right now."

"OK, OK, how about this then? Penny for my thoughts?" June said, pointing towards his right temple. This always got Rico's attention. Like most crackheads, June was the consistent victim of dealers and abuse from the neighborhood teens. He got picked on and slapped around. Black used to throw firecrackers in the alleyway June slept in just to see him run out. Rico, however, always tried to treat June with some dignity. Rico's mother once told him that June used to be a schoolteacher before his wife and son were killed in a car accident. She said he'd died with them, but his body lived on, and every now and then for a brief second, he'd present bits of wisdom. So, Rico began giving him a dollar whenever June would say "Penny for my thoughts." Which was a lot since Rico could tell that June hadn't been sober long. His humor and enthusiasm spoke of a man without a care in the world.

"What you got for me, June Bug?" Rico said, holding out a dollar

"Did you know a dead man can kill you just as fast as a man that's breathing?"

"What do you mean?" Rico replied

"Shit, I don't know, read it somewhere. Anyways I need some liquor and some pussy. Peace in the Middle East Rico!" And just like that, he was gone. Rico continued towards the Quick Trip gas station. Old June's words seemed prophetic, but Rico didn't have time to decipher the words of a crackhead trying to earn a dollar. Liquor and pussy were two things Rico couldn't really afford. The effects of alcohol were evident in people like JD and June Bug. Rico found it amusing that people celebrated success with champagne and all that fancy Cristal and shit. Why punctuate your high point with a depressant? It seemed like rich people celebrated good times by inviting bad ones. Rico wasn't with that, but life on Lincoln Way had a way of making you contradict your own beliefs. He didn't have Cristal money, but he wasn't above an occasional taste of E and J. "Erk and Jerk," "Ease Us Jesus" It went by lots of names, but more importantly, it went cheap and got the job done.

Pussy was likewise a complex luxury in Rico's life. While alcohol could send you to a homeless shelter, pussy could send you to the graveyard. Women were the unwitting grim reapers of Lincoln Way: touching the wrong could mean death. It was hard to tell which women were fair game with all the pimps and hotheaded dope boys in the area. On top of that, the women that were spoken for were the ones that would *always* make themselves available. Rico wondered why they seemed to love drama knowing they're the least likely to suffer the consequences. Tanisha got Black killed. The streets said that it was one big setup. Something about Chis, Black, and another guy. She was only fucking him to make her baby's father, Chris, jealous. Word is Chris, and Black killed each other. Now Rico missed Black

To hell with Chris. Tanisha hasn't been seen since, but if and when she pops up, Rico's got one of Black's hollow points waiting on her.

Alanna used to be Rico's girl, but she was rarely there. Her flightiness led to their breakup ... Well, that and her alcoholism. Rico couldn't understand why she didn't love herself as much as she loved him. Maybe they'll talk when she returns from rehab. Maybe. Either Chantel or Monica was almost always available with their legs or mouths open until then. Maybe they weren't hoes in the traditional sense, but neither one of them ever ran from a dick. Rico knew he'd have a better chance at seeing one of them run for president than running from some dick. That suited Rico just fine for the time being. Maybe after his meeting was done, he'd call Chantel up for some fun.

Thoughts of sex quickly disappeared once the QT came into view. The pumps were empty, and Rico could see that the clerk was on his break. He noticed the parking spots were empty except for one vehicle as he approached. Upon first inspection, it looked like an SUV, maybe a jeep, but he realized it was a Range Rover as he casually passed by. Rico had seen a Range Rover Sport or two in his lifetime but never a high-end full-sized Range. The vehicle looked as if it had arrived fresh from the land of video vixens and jewelry stores, yet Rico knew this was the guy he was here to see. Rico continued past the gas station and around the corner. Anyone that's ever been jumped knows you always case a meeting before you make a meeting. A passing glance told Rico everything he wanted to know. The bright white vehicle had Maryland plates. Whoever owned it was from out of town unless it was a rental. Snow didn't stick well to the paint or the glass, so it's been well-kept with wax and rain-X. The rims were stock Land Rover Alloys. No aftermarket wheels. It had to belong to someone over 40.

Most importantly, there were two people in the vehicle: one in the driver seat and one behind him. That meant they intended Rico to get into the passenger seat with a possible gun-toting stranger behind him. Not going to happen. This was a setup. Rico palmed the gun in his jacket pocket and turned out of sight of the QT. Why would that second person be in the backseat unless—

"Just like your pop," said a voice from the corner ahead of him.

"You read the situation first before you made a commitment, but tell me, did you ever consider that there were three people in that vehicle?" Said the stranger that resembled Ron Isely stepping out of the shadows.

Saying nothing, Rico aimed silver at the stranger.

"I'm not here to hurt you, Youngblood," said Ron holding his hands up. At that same moment Rico's right eye began to react to a bright red flash.

He played with laser pointers as a child and recognized his reaction.

"I'm not here to hurt you, but if you want to get hurt, keep aiming that pistol at me."

Mr. Isely's words made him realize that Rico wasn't a step ahead in this situation. He was a step behind. He also realized he wasn't being harassed by a laser pointer but by an infrared laser sight on a gun pointed at him from some undisclosed location. After a brief pause, he lowered his gun.

"What do you want?" he said, feeling exposed.

"I only want to talk to you. I'm a businessman, and I worked with your father. He owned a building, and now, if you like, it's yours. Or it could be anyway, if you're ready. Don't make any rash decisions just yet. I wanted to take you over to see for yourself, but I knew you'd be suspicious and try to find a setup. It's what your father would have done."

Rico thought for a moment. He didn't like the idea of being compared to his absent father or the twinge of child-like pride he felt at the sound of it. He didn't like being set up either, but he'd be dead already if these guys wanted to shoot him. He didn't own anything of value, so this wasn't robbery or extortion. Fuck it. He couldn't think of any real reasons not to hear the man out. Worst case scenario: he could sell the "building." He might not make out of this situation alive it if anything stupid happened, but neither would Uncle Ron. "How far are we talking about?"

two
naughty girl

THERE'S something unwelcoming about an empty house at 6 AM. A young woman's home is her sanctuary. It's the place she can wipe off her make-up, take off uncomfortable shoes and accessories, throw on some relaxing music and enjoy a warm shower. The warmth of a shower is a penetrating one. It's not just about being clean; it's about being reborn in your original flesh with the toxins and memories of a long day sliding from your body and disappearing down the drain, never to be seen or heard from again. Intoxicating washes and lotions mask the smell of sweat and dirt and regret and hatted. The aromatic cloud can whisk you away, clothed in a warm lather. It's the luxury of a brief reprieve from the endless self-reflection of the woman you've become. This is a routine of comfort, a baptism of self appreciation in a world that could never appreciate you or the services you provide in the night for the pleasure of strangers.

Once all is said and done, the cloud dissipates. The scent lingers, clinging to you as if to remind you and inform the world you've been cleansed. You are again pure and are at peace to find yourself wrapped in the grace in which you move about your sanctuary. The only trace of evidence against your feminine virtue is the lingering stain near the shower drain. It lingers there impossibly resistant against cleaners in scrubs. It stares at you, reminding you of the eyes. The same eyes that

9

fall upon you as you enter someone's world only to be paid filthy by it. The eyes stare at you with a cold expectation and a dark desire so intense that you can't differentiate a smile from a look of bitter contempt. Like the shower's steam, the eyes watch you leave with full knowledge of your most intimate secrets. You've been exploited, and no amount of fantasy-inducing soaps will ever completely purify you, not even in your own sanctuary.

Sienna was all too familiar with the cycle of innocence and exploitation. It was a festering wound she'd learn to live with ... for now. As she stepped into the house, the question on her mind was, where is Rico? It wasn't like him to stay out all night. Since Alanna left for rehab, he hasn't had a good reason, and Brandon was killed over that girl Tanisha. Sienna wondered with a twinge of panic if Rico had finally found out the truth about her, where she went, and the things she did.

"No, not possible," she told herself as she began to remove her make-up and earrings. As she sat in her room staring at the mirror, she couldn't help but notice how ridiculously overdressed she was. Here she was in one of the run-down sections of Lincoln-Way dressed as if she had just returned from the red carpet. She couldn't help but thank her mother for her good genes when she looked at herself. Caramel skin, jet black hair, brown eyes, and a toned curved body responded to exercise and diet twice as fast as her girlfriends. As she walked through the kitchen, she noticed a box of pop tarts hastily opened and a wrapper still on the table. When your work requires you to be in and out of strange men's homes, you notice the details. You never knew when someone's wife or, worse, their kids might show up unexpectedly. Sienna knew the gentleman from the slobs, although, could any of them really be considered a gentleman if they needed her services? Rico was no slob, so he must have left in a hurry. Was Food Shark open this early? Sienna was a night hawk, she didn't have a clue.

Sienna wouldn't be surprised to see Rico leaving extra early for work. He'd always been hard-working. She knew he was grinding his way to a managerial position so they could live more comfortably. Rico tried to play it straight, but he knew the street almost as well as she did. She could remember once when some junky tried to break into their house. Rico pulled a gun she didn't even know he owned and shot inches away from the window the fiend tried to come through. He didn't want to kill the guy and didn't even realize he was doing them all a favor. The fiend lived to rob another day; Rico was a hero, and Sienna didn't have to reveal to her brother that she had her *own* gun and would have shot the fool herself. She didn't want her brother to know she carried. A girl's got to look after herself. A week later, she'd gone out looking for protection against such dangers to her or her brother. After giving a few people some special favors, she had not only acquired a new provocative yet secret lifestyle, but she also put her home on the permanent protection list. She sold her soul to protect her home, but Rico didn't need to know that. Rico needed to be the good man he was ... for the both of them.

As she picked out her clothes, Sienna heard the familiar buzz of her phone coming from her coat on the chair.

"What the hell?" was all she could say in protest before reading the text.

/ CLEO NEED U 2 BE @ 1201 4th STREET ALLEY THE LATEST CLIENT NEEDS TO BE SHOWN SOME LOVE BUT DOESN'T WANT YOU TO BE SEEN/

"Love?" She thought. "Pfft," what she provided wasn't "love" at all. She gave them what they needed, and sometimes she hated herself for it.

/I'M OFF THE CLOCK/ was her only plea of defiance.

/20 MINUTES/ was the only response, but it was enough to tell her she had no choice in the matter. This wasn't a request; these were instructions. There was no response except compliance or consequences.

"Fucking pimp," Sienna spat to no one but herself. She washed quickly (So much for a soul-cleansing experience) and found something tight and black to wear. She looked like a black rose and felt like a used car. Before she left the sanctuary, her last thoughts were about Rico's whereabouts at this time of the morning.

Cleo emerged from the house of Sienna and Rico as she had done many nights before. She moved silently and quickly with a poisonous seduction that filled the air around her. She was focused and moved with a purpose. She had no illusions about what she was about to do. She was, once again, going to be used. She was already moving at the behest of her master through the snow and pleasure-defying chill of Lincoln Way. She would use this time to build confidence. She would tell herself she wasn't being used; she was using them. They may have soiled her soul, but they could never have it completely. Her mind and body were hers alone. They had to pay her with money and protection, and connections. By this time next year, she and Rico could move away from Lincoln-Way with the money she'd saved. She wasn't just some lady of the night; she *was* the night. They needed her. She allowed herself to be used this way to achieve her own ends. She had the beauty of Nefertiti and the Power of Isis. It was Cleopatra.

"Uh-Oh, watch out now!" her thoughts were interrupted by none other than old June. She kept moving as he struggled to keep up.

"Why does someone so pretty always look so tired?" He spoke. She could smell a hint of Thunderbird on his breath as he struggled to keep pace. Maybe Night train?

"I'm sorry, June bug, but I have to meet someone soon."

"Oh no!" he said, clutching his chest, "love of my life done shot me down for another man, all in a night's work, I guess," he said, sitting in the snow feigning injury.

This made her pause; she couldn't help but smile at the antics of this okie fool. She wondered if his words had meaning but quickly dismissed it as the rantings of a walking tragedy. "Did he say shut me down or shot me down?" Who knows? June was a sweet old guy, plus she knew his story.

"Here, June Bug, now I've got to go," she said, handing him a dollar.

"If you think my love can be bought... you're absolutely right!" He said, quickly stuffing the bill in his pants pocket.

"If pretty women walk the mean streets, do the streets become pretty, or are it the other way around?" June said in a sobering moment of clarity.

"What do you mean by that—"

"And Iiiieeeyyiiieeeeyiliii will always love you," he sang in a poor rendition of the classic Whitney Houston song as he went back the way he came. Cleo had no time to waste deciphering his code. She had to go get that money and be on time.

When she approached the alley, she could see her employer's vehicle just out of sight. She couldn't believe she was being reduced to working in a squalid alley. The presence of a large green dumpster didn't exactly make her feel like the Queen of the Nile. She stood there out of sight as instructed, waiting for her cue. Her manager rarely made his presence known, so seeing him there told her she was being watched. She knew what to do. She was familiar with the ways of the flesh, so to speak. It's too cold for bullshit, and he's fucking up her relaxation time. Her phone buzzes, and she picks it up and reads:

/YOU'LL KNOW HIM WHEN YOU SEE HIM. HE'LL BE NERCOUS CAUSE IT' HIS FIRST TIME. DON'T TOUCH HIM UNLESS YOU HAVE TO/

"Don't touch him? Yeah, right," she thinks. "When have I ever had a client that didn't get touched?" She began to see movement in the distance. It was mister-get-your-ass-to-a-dark-alley himself. He was joined by another man. Probably the one she was supposed to meet in the alley. Bastard's got her waiting in the cold like he's some sort of superstar. Maybe he is. Maybe this is the jackpot she's been waiting on. She quickly applies her make-up. She could hardly recognize herself. She does a last-minute check of her toy bag. Everything there as it should be: A modified Surgeon 591 Short Action Sniper Rifle, pistol gripped RMB-93 Shotgun, A 10 round Desert Eagle III, 20 yards of 550 cord, a medical kit, and a soldering iron. God only knows what this client will ask for. Then suddenly, as if he'd read her mind, he asked for it. He pointed a pistol at the manager she's been sent here to protect. She quickly reaches into her bag and pulls out the sniper rifle. It's a beautiful work with the inscribed designation .591 LUV inscribed on the magazine well. This guy has a gun pointed at her employer. She shines infrared light in his face long enough to distract him and allow her to be ready for the kill shot Another night, another soon-to-be dead body. Another shower to clean the death from her soul.

As she prepares to serve this guy and dirty herself once again, she begins to control her breathing. Accuracy is all in the breath and grip. As she readies the kill shot, she looks through the scope; she freezes at the sight of Rico holding a gun on her employer ... then lowering it. She can say nothing as she watches the two men get into the Range Rover and drive away. She receives a text as she removes the black eye makeup and black lipstick.

/GOOD JOB/

/FUCK YOU/

/I TOLD YOU NOT TO TOUCH HIM. I TRUSTED YOU TO FOLLOW INSTRUCTIONS. ITS TIME TO MAKE HIM THE MAN HE WAS MEANT TO BE. HE'S SAFE./

/HE BETTER BE. NEXT TIME I BETTER HAVE MORE INFO/

/YOU WILL CLEO YOU WILL/

This bastard has me out all night like some kind of hooker, Cleo thinks as she heads home. But I'm Cleopatra, a beautiful death and more than most men deserve. She can't help but laugh at herself for sounding like a cartoon character. Humor is one of the most important tools an assassin has in their arsenal other than guns. The walk home was long and confusing. Does Rico know that she's a hitwoman? No, he'd never come to that conclusion. He probably just thinks she's a hoe. She chuckles at the thought. "Like anyone could put a price on all this. Please, I'll snap necks before I turn tricks; I'm Cleo bitch. They better know what I'm about." As she approached the house, Cleopatra opened the door and faded away as Sienna stepped into the familiar and hopefully temporary surroundings. Now about that shower ...

three
sky's the limit

ON LINCOLN WAY, WORDS LIKE "LUXURY" or "elegance" are as elusive as words like "justice" or "success." Here there are very few luxuries that exist and those that do are small and short-lived. An expensive pair of shoes or designer mobile phone is usually the most residents can afford to claim as a luxury. No one would care how refined your new watch is even in these situations. If the watch is nice that it's "tough" or "hard," nobody gives a fuck about pretty words. Save that for CNN. The highest compliments belie the aesthetics of an item and instead promote its durability. In the streets, survival and durability are of the utmost importance. The weak and soft are routinely destroyed by the strong in this world. There's no room for Brooks Brothers slacks, only LevI's denim. Patten leather tears easily on broken glass, but construction boots easily negotiate even the most dangerous terrain. If you "go hard" or you're "cold" at something, it means that you're admired for your ruthless efficiency. If you're a pussy... Well, the next hard motherfucker is going to take you down. No, there's no room for luxury or elegance, but these are the only words Rico could use to describe the interior of the vehicle he had just entered.

Rico desperately tried not to be distracted by the obviously expensive leather seats. The music was a track he recognized. "Void Walker" by Ayokipp was familiar to him, but the sound was so pure and clean he thought that for the very first time in his life, he could actually hear the emotions in what the guy was saying. The engine was so quiet Rico had to wonder if this thing was powered by normal gasoline. Did Range Rover make hybrids? Rico didn't know. The only intrusive sound he could hear from his rear passenger seat position was the sound of Mr. Isely texting on his cell phone. Rico couldn't help but be curious about who was on the other end of the text, but he let that thought go for now.

Rico could hardly see the driver's face, but the rearview mirror allowed him to see his eyes. The guy had slightly cocked eyes Rico hated that because it made them hard to read. There was no use in eliciting a response because the driver was completely focused on the road. "Obedient," Rico thought, "that's bad news." The only way a man would be obedient to another is if the other has money, power, or both. The man beside Rico looked like he was at least 6'3 as far as Rico could tell and black as night. His large frame was more "fat" than "muscle," but it was enough to make Rico glad to have silver with him. This guy's body language said the sloth, but his eyes gave away the sneaky nature of this behemoth. Rico could tell from the guy's build and body language that he was made to look like the muscle, but he was as soft as the leather of the rover seats. He's too big to be a con artist Rico mused. Maybe a thief or a gambler. He was trying to make a sale, but Rico wasn't buying.

"Managing real talent is a chore," Uncle Ron lamented, interrupting Rico's train of thought.

"Where are we going?" That was all Rico could think to say "The CABAL" was all Mr. Isely said.

He may as well have said The White House or the fucking Batcave as far as Rico was concerned.

The Cesar and Brutus Alliance Lounge was probably the most intimidating building downtown. Rico had never been inside, but he knew it held a nightclub, a few suits, and several floors of white-collar business. Most of the parking was underground, so you rarely saw anyone enter the front door of the building. The building posted dozens of windows, none of which you could pier through from ground level. Monica used to drive Uber and sometimes pick people up from the nightclub. She always talked about how bougie the scene was and didn't understand why anyone would buy all those expensive clothes and makeup just to go out. She'd never do that. Rico thought that was close enough to the truth: she'd never do that because she'd never get the opportunity. She was simply too ratchet. A cool girl to kick it with but no class, so you couldn't take her anywhere. She wasn't afraid to lay on her back at the drop of a hat for Rico, which told him she probably treated every guy like that. He could tell by the way she described the place that she'd fantasized about being a member. Now Rico found himself headed there at the crack of dawn.

"Do you work there or what?" Rico asked, thinking about the prospect of a new job.

"I don't work anywhere. I work *for* people and *through* places. Remember that."

Mr. Isely's response sounded like some James Bond mystery shit to Rico. The secrecy was getting old, but he decided to play along. After all, they let him keep silver when they could have easily disarmed him. Whatever they wanted from him, they wanted him to be as comfortable as possible. If things went sideways, he could pop a hole in fat boy and Ron Isely before Cockeye could slam on the brakes.

The SUV descended the ramp leading to the parking garage below the building. They descended into the darkness of the lot as dawn approached. Rico only got a glimpse of the morning sun, it felt like they were somehow running from the daylight itself. Rico was surprised to find a car detail shop nestled in the labyrinth of parking spaces. "Dope," he thought. It was a perfect place to get high-priced vehicles and generously tipping customers. Rico always wondered in these situations who had the upper hand? The customer that demands convenience, or the service provider supplying that convenience at an elevated cost. Supply and demand. It's all some kind of game, but there is a price to play just like any game. And Rico was typically too broke for anything other than the occasional video game.

"Well, we're here. I'm sure you've heard about this place and all the business that goes on here. You must understand that the CABAL has two faces. The shining smile of the night and the cold stare of the day. The environment and atmosphere attract money and power to places like this. This place has many levels, and the gears are always turning to rise above those levels. That's the hustle... a corporate hustle. The particulars of each business don't even matter as much as the aura they give off. A million-dollar idea can sound like bullshit coming from a crack head. Trump says, "Let's build a wall to keep out the Mexicans," and people eat it up knowing it's probably the stupidest thing a sitting president has ever said. It's all about environment and atmosphere. It's about presenting the perfect image to keep the business going."

"If this hustle is so corporate, why are you picking me up before business hours on the wrong side of town like you're smuggling El Chappo?" Rico asked, challenging the idyllic speech.

"That's a good question, but do my actions take away from anything I've said? You're paying attention, but you're not listening. Every action illustrates a point. You look around Lincoln Way, and you see everyone trying to find a way to survive. Those who have mastered basic survival are trying to find any way to prosper beyond survival. No one is born dishonest; few are born brilliant. Everyone is born with instinct. What separates you from your Food Shark staff? Time, Experience, Skill? Nope, it's instinct. That's it. Your instinct to prosper will drive you to learn the skills and build the temple. There's instinct... then there's blind luck. You can always rely on one of the two, but just remember instincts can be wrong, and luck can be bad."

Ron steps out of the vehicle, and Rico follows his lead. The semi-packed parking lot was a labyrinth that led to several elevator shafts. Half of the floors on the digital keypad had locks on them when they approached the right pad Mr. Isely pressed one and typed in a code. 8-7-3-... damn. Rico wasn't quick enough to get the last number, but he knew most of it. He'd have to log that into his memory. Who knows when he'd need it.

As the elevator descended, Rico asked, "What's your name? We've gone a long way, and I never got your name."

"Prescott... you can call me Mr. Prescott. The two men with me are Marshall and Adonis, the driver," the man said without turning to look.

Well, that was easy enough. Why didn't he just say that from the jump? Was he testing Rico to see how long it would take him to ask? Was he gauging his limits?

Rico was finally getting over the elegance of the garage and trying to imagine what he was walking into. A lifetime of actions movies told him that he was either walking into some huge drug operation or Men in Black headquarters. Nah... too many black people for a government operation. All the affirmative action in the world wouldn't have four black agents in the same place on the same operation. What if his father had enemies? (Father...) What if this was organized for him to be killed like Joe Pecci in Good fellas? He was getting well-known at Food Shark, but not quite elaborate-gangland execution material. The thought of it almost made him laugh to himself until he remembered the laser pointer incident. He had to stay sharp. This whole situation was sweet and sour at the same time. Not knowing how to feel gave him an uneasiness that made him glad to have Silver close by.

Speaking of uneasy feelings, where the hell was Sienna? Rico thought to reach for his phone, but he hadn't felt any vibrations from it, and he wasn't sure if anyone would realize that he still had it on him. He didn't want to make any moves that would raise suspicions or tighten security. Sienna probably assumed he was at Food Shark, so she wouldn't be worried about where he was for a while ... assuming she was home.

four
more than a woman

Your love is a One in a Million. It goes on and on and on …
Your love is a One in a Million. It goes on and on and on …
Your love is a Click!

"I KNOW, GIRL. … " Sienna responded to her cell phone alarm. The abrupt ending of the Aaliyah classic seemed to be a direct reflection of the sudden ending of the trancelike state of Sienna's deep sleep. That's one reason she's kept the same alarm for so long. The tragedy of the singer's untimely death meant that her music was frozen in time at the peak of its impact. They aren't classic songs. That implies that they've aged. They're songs that never erode or lose their potency. They always feel brand new. The familiarity of the disruption was almost a comfort. The soothing sounds and words that are romantic and, at the same time, encouraging can give a person the right mind state with which to face the day. The fact is that people depend on music to identify themselves. The masterful expression of emotion, struggle, confidence, triumph, and vulnerability doesn't come easy to the average person. That's why music has such a hold on humanity. The sounds have an almost drug-like effect on a person's emotions, and the words find a way to both speak to the listener and, at the same time, speak for the listener. It's the most intimate experience that everyone shares to some degree without a sense of jealousy or entitlement. The few gatekeepers and hardcore music fans are only snobs because they don't believe you're enjoying the music *enough*. It's not that you shouldn't enjoy it but that you shouldn't enjoy it if you don't understand its depth and subtle meaning. Sienna was different; still, she knew what it meant: Time to get up.

Looking at her phone, she saw 3 Missed Calls. Asia called twice. Laura once and to top it all off, a WYD text from Devin. Sienna hated WYD text. Something about being texted instead of called felt so shallow and dismissive.

She met Devin while out with her girls. She didn't even want to go, but it was Asia's birthday, and she ALWAYS wanted to go out. It was almost like she was looking for something in the sights and sounds of the nightclubs. It wasn't guys; it wasn't even the drinks; it was something else that kept calling her back into the world of fabricated fun. Whatever it was, it always required Laura, Nicole, and Sienna to accompany her. Nicole was cool as long as she could drink, and a bitch didn't look at her the wrong way. Sienna can't remember when a bitch didn't look a Nicole the wrong way. Sometimes Sienna wondered if Nicole was so eager to fight all the time because the guys were never looking at her the *right* way. Poor girl just wanted attention even if she had to beat a bitch up for it. Laura was a sweetheart; she was always cool and calm, a pretty smoker girl. She was also Boo'd up. Going out with your girls is always fun until the one girl who volunteered to drive decides she misses her man and is ready to return home. It was like, who would rather be at home hugged up on some guy than go out? Sienna would, that's who. Laura was lucky because she had a guy she wanted to go home to.

Who did Sienna have? Rico, her brother, and a magic wand personal massager when she was alone. Sure, there are plenty of guys out there, but none that were impressive enough to spend any real time with, plus she didn't want to be one of those hoes running around like Chantel and Monica. Sometimes Sienna wondered if that would be more fun. Why else would they live like that? But nah fuck that. Sienna had too much pride to just be with anybody. She wanted to eventually have someone with quality, and she wanted to make sure she was the type of woman only a quality man wanted to be with. Plus, she needed a man that would understand her...work ...

Devin was definitely unqualified. He was cute and all, but Sienna is 24, not 12. Devin was 25 but he seemed to be another Instagram flexing wannabe. At first, he seemed to have some depth to him especially standing next to his friends. He broke away from the pack and offered Sienna a drink. Classic move. The type of thing a gentleman would do. At least that's how Sienna thought gentlemen moved. She didn't have a dad to know, and her mother rarely brought any men around her and her brother. When Devin started asking her about herself, she felt more nervous than expected. Was this a good thing? So much for Cleo Queen of the night... by the end of the night, she gave him her number and began to wonder if this might *go* somewhere. Welp, it did ... and it stayed there for 4 days because that's how long it took him to hit her up. Bump that.

As Sienna freshened up and ate some cereal, she realized that Rico still wasn't home. Her mind raced through the night. She'd nearly forgotten about almost shooting her brother. Somebody was going to have to answer for that. Maybe Mr. Prescott thinks she's to be toyed with, but he should know better than that. He should know better than to cross Cle...

"If at first you don't succeed, dust yourself off and try again," her phone rang.

So, she's an Aaliyah fan, so what? "Hello"

"Hey Bitch," Asia said on the other line

"Hey Girl, I saw your call. I was about to hit you up once I got finished eating."

"Yeah yeah, yo ass was probably not going to be finished until 8 o'clock tomorrow night then."

Sienna couldn't help but laugh. Asia's energy was always so infectious that you'd find yourself laughing before you knew it.

"I told you before you should get me Rico's number, and that way, I could call him when I'm trying to reach you." She tried it.

"I think not because I'd have to burn down your house and you'd be stuck living with me. I don't need you or your light skin makeup clogging up our bathroom."

Asia laughed this time. "Ok ... I was just playing"

After a brief conversation, it was decided that they'd meet up and

22

grab some lunch. It seemed like a normal enough plan. Sienna valued normalcy as much as safety. Normalcy was a rare commodity that she reached for but could rarely grasp end even then ... never fully. It didn't take long to shower and dress. She was just grabbing her keys when the door opened, and Rico stepped in so lost in thought he barely noticed her.

"Um ... hey," Sienna asked, hiding her concern by pretending to be annoyed.

"What's up ... my bad, I took half a day. I didn't really feel up to working, know what I mean? I'm surprised you're here. I didn't even see you last night... what you been up to," he said, making eye contact.

Sienna found herself on the back foot. He'd prepared for this. Rico was always a quick thinker, especially when it came to dialogue and debate. He could reverse any situation and throw you off your game. He'd lied to her in a way she couldn't readily expose and, in the same breath, forced her to lie to him even if through omission.

"I came in late. You must have been sleeping," she attempted to reverse the situation without meeting his gaze. "Anyway, I'm headed out with Asia to grab some lunch. I'll be back tonight if you want me to grab you some dinner."

"That's what's up," he responded. "Be safe out there and tell Asia I eat lunch too," he said jokingly.

"Boy, Asia is not paying you no attention. Anyways I'll hit you when I'm on my way back to see if you're still here." As she headed to the door, she realized something had been bothering her since Rico got home. Something subtle but subconsciously noticeable. She couldn't place it during their conversation, and now that she was past him, she didn't want to start hovering over him. As she closed the front door, it hit her. Was he wearing new shoes?

five
cellz

RICO KNEW how to carry himself when he entered an unfamiliar place. It's all about the emotional extremes. Never be too excited. Never be too nervous. Never be too anything. Take everything in stride. He wasn't about to let his mental training fail him as he entered the first floor of the CABAL, but it wasn't an easy task.

The nightclub was empty at this time of the morning, but Rico could tell it was everything he'd imagined. It looked like all the best parts of an early 2000's music video. Black marble floors with white accents and gold fixtures. An elevated platform cut halfway through the center of the place used as a stage. A deep glass dance floor surrounded by a layer of high-end poker and roulette tables. Rico didn't play cards, but he knew that the wages were in the thousands to play here. People die over $50 dice games in Lincoln way. He wondered what they'd do over the thousands at stake in here.

Outside the Gambling tables were a two-tear stadium seating of dining tables. If you were at a table, you could dine and enjoy whatever you wanted to see just out of arms' reach. The temptation to leave your table to participate in the dancing and gambling had to be enormous. Near the ceiling opposite the center stage was a short series of booths. It looked like the owner's box from a football game to Rico. He knew whoever sat there had to be invite only. Imagine what kind of juice a person had to have to comfortably gaze down on the people like an Olympian God. To look down and catch the inevitable stare of a patron below and silently declare your station above their own. The implied contempt for the unwashed masses was clear because there were no direct steps leading to these booths. They could dominate this realm with perfect majesty without ever touching the floor.

"We can stop back though here on the way down if you want," Mr. Prescott said, amused.

Rico hadn't even noticed that he'd stopped to stare. He'd betrayed himself in that brief moment by giving away his quiet awe. He could only imagine how many people had been just as seduced by this place. How many had succumbed to gambling, infidelity, addiction ... all because they were in a luxurious trance they'd hoped would last forever.

He'd regained his demeanor and began walking behind Mr. Prescott, hoping that his pause hadn't been embarrassingly long. After taking another elevator and walking on a circular floor, they finally arrived at an office. It was vast and had a fantastic view of downtown, but it paled in comparison to the fantasy land downstairs. Prescott had an L-shaped desk with a few computer monitors on one side and various documents on the other. This was clearly designed so that he could take meetings face to face. Rico half expected to see a taxidermy bear in the corner of the large office a la C. Montgomery Burns. No such luck.

Prescott gave a gesture with his eyes, and Rico could hear Adonis and Marshall retreat outside the office. Prescott then pulled out a diagram, unrolled it across the desk, and presented it to Rico in a way that seemed practiced. The diagram contained Club, Recording Studio, Conference Rooms, Gym, Office Space, Penthouses.

"This is the CABAL. This is everything that makes the city run. Each section represents a part of the totality of the people's interest in one way or another. See, we have maintained certain structural integrity by making sure that there are no issues when dealing with our partners, and that allows us to operate in a way that benefits ourselves and anyone we find valuable."

"Well, if you're looking to take over Food Shark and need an inside guy, then you're gonna be pissed when you hear I was recently fired," Rico said sarcastically.

Prescott smiled and continued, "The problem is that occasionally we need new blood and fresh ideas to generate a consistent flow of interest in what we have going here. Young people ... not kids, of course, but the 20-30-year- old demographic. Let me back up ... until today; what came to mind when you looked at the CABAL? What did you think about it?"

Rico thought for a moment. "I really never saw it, but it's one of those places people lie about getting into. Everybody has a friend that works there or dated someone that did. It's a mix of a music video and Sodom or Gomorrah. Or maybe it's just a business. Everybody knows about the club, but no one asks or talks about anything else in the building."

"Good. That's what we want to keep a certain allure about the place. The CABAL is basically a conglomerate of self-interested businesses that form a body. Each level operates like a system. The essential functions started like interdependent organs. The recording studio feeds artists to the Club. The artist and club need legal representation, so the club pays for the lawyers and so forth. You follow me?"

"Yeah, I get what you're saying; without one, the others can't exist for long. That's all dope. Very smooth. But why are you showing and telling me all this? What's the point of bringing me here?" Rico asked, hoping to get a handle on all the presented information.

"Well, think of me as the brain or at least the heart of this functioning body. I make sure we get enough food, water, and air to forever reproduce, grow and expand. Isn't that want everybody needs."

"Yeah, and protection and the ability to reproduce," Rico said, keeping pace.

"See, that's why I fuck with you, young blood. You've been here five minutes, and you already seem smarter than you did on the phone."

Rico noticed the backhanded compliment and couldn't tell if it was maliciousness or dry wit. Old Black folks can be like that sometimes. You can't tell if they're picking with you or picking on you.

"The reason you're here is that if each level of the CABAL is an organ, then each person here is a cell. Cells keep shit operating, and there are times when we need fresh new cells. Your father was a pioneer. He damn near took the town over and knocked down anything that stood in his way. Gentrification, politics, white folks, gangs, loan sharks."

"Family, his children, anything that got in the way of his bag, right" Rico was starting to feel himself going from impressed to irritated.

"I get it. I can't speak for him or explain why I'm just now reaching out to you. He kept his personal situations private. It was his business. That's it. It wasn't my place to ask who he did what with and when. I had my own shit to worry about, and no offense, you weren't on my list."

Rico could tell Mr. Prescott wasn't going to be begging forgiveness on behalf of his late father.

"So that cell died now you want a new one? Is that where this is going? You want me to spread the word?"

What a waste of time. All this extra secret service bullshit just for a recruitment speech about the club looking for more people or maybe a job working as a bar back or some shit? Rico wasn't feeling the situation now and suddenly felt like he was a thousand miles from home and realized no one knew where he was. It was time to make a mental breakdown of what he knew: Prescott worked for or with his dad and knew his mother. Prescott owns or at least has a high position in the CABAL. He's got at least 2 security guards with him, probably right outside the door. He was confident enough to allow Rico to keep his gun after showing him it would likely be of little use with the whole dark alley shooter situation. No real way to make it out alive if shit goes left. Better dial back that tone a little bit.

"No, quite the opposite. I'm offering you an internship. You would work here at the CABAL for me as a rep in my absence. You come from a good breed, and we need to mix things up here. Plus, I owe your dad that, at least. What, are you afraid you can't hack it? Please, don't tell me you're a fish out of water. I did my homework. Solid grades in HS and the only one among your known friends to graduate with honors... or at all, for that matter.

"Scholarship offers to Howard, Emory, Auburn, Samford ... and a clean record. Your name has been in four separate police statements, including a drug bust. People were arrested. In one situation, a man was killed. Somehow, you've never been a suspect of anything. No real record of criminal activity or being a police informant. Nothing. Yet you were comfortable enough to leave your house at 0'dark thirty, talk to a crackhead, assess a meeting point, and carry with you an unregistered weapon. You're even practiced at attempting to hide your thoughts and emotions behind a veneer of attitude and confidence. Where do you pick up movements and habits like that? The mean streets of Food Shark? N ah, you're good at adapting and evolving, from what I can tell. Do you know what kind of cell makes you? A brain cell."

There was a silence that passed between them. The verbal sparring match gave way to a lesson, maybe even mentorship. Their eyes connected, and faces remained stoic. Rico knew he'd been researched, but that didn't explain why. The more pressing concern was how long he'd been watched. If Mr. Prescott just started doing his homework when his father died, then that's some quick research. If he'd been tracking Rico before that, then his story of happening to need new blood right now was bullshit. Either way, Rico's mind couldn't help wondering what this meant as far as an opportunity. An internship at the CABAL? Rico refused to let his mind get distracted by the implied prospects of power and influence that come from being associated with a place like that.

"So, you seem to be a lot like 'my father.' You said he gets obstacles out of the way. It sounds to me like you've put me in a position where I can't say no."

Prescott's deadpan grimace gave way to a half-smile.

"You got rid of my job before contacting me, convinced me to walk outside of my neighborhood at a time most people are asleep, threatened me with a gun added to the threat by being unbothered about me keeping my own, now you have me ducked off in a place no one will think to look to find me so you can propose to offer me an internship ... a paid internship I bet."

"Of course."

"Well ... when do I start?" Rico said, resigned to see what happened next.

"Immediately," Mr. Prescott said, pressing a button without breaking eye contact, Adonis brings him some shoes."

six

how's it going down

Sometime back...

"DEVOTION AND NOTHING LESS. That's what people expect from each other in a relationship. That's the way to be just me and you. You don't understand shawty. I be trying to fuck with you, but you know a nigga gonna be a nigga. Long as I bring it all back to you, I'm yours and you mine shiiit we straight. Shit don't last forever that why you gotta be devoted to a real nigga. Niggas gon' play but that shit ain't serious. These nothing ass hoes don't mean shit for real. Most time when I go out who do I have with me? Especially when it's something important?"

Sienna has heard it a thousand times. At this point, it just becomes white noise. It's not Bolo's cheating or rough nature that surprised her anymore; it was the fact that she still cried after all this time. How could her emotions and body betray her over and over again? Bolo was the typical "Trap nigga" or "real nigga" or whatever the phrase was these days. In High School, he was so much different. At least it seemed that way. Was she stupid then or what?

All the girls wanted Bolo because he was a dope boy. He had fly shit on all the time. He only ever really came to school so people could see him walk out halfway through the day. She couldn't really say what it was. He wasn't really handsome in the classic sense, but he had a certain ruggedness that was sexy. He was a rebel not confined by the "rules." He was getting it however he wanted. That means he would give you all the nice shoes and dinner dates, and you could ride around in his car with the speakers bumping and feel like that bitch. Sienna knew men thought of women as accessories, but she always thought of guys as elaborate chauffeurs. Give me gifts, take me places, make these hoes jealous, while I make these fools jealous of you. Tell me what I want to hear, make me feel good, and then thank me for the opportunity. Do that, and then we can all pretend you have the power. That's what it meant to have a dope boy for a boyfriend. It all seemed to work out pretty well most times. Sure, there were these wannabe little girls that thought if they sucked his dick enough, he'd trade up, but he knew better than to leave Sienna up for grabs.

Sienna was in great shape (thank you for two years of basketball and one Cheer squad), and Momma made her thick in all the right places. No, she wouldn't be in any music videos, but she could probably stroll her way on TV or a Movie if it fit. These clowns were in her inbox all the time talking shit about each other, trying to win her favor. She would usually pawn them off on her homegirls if they were cute enough. She knew she looked good enough that she didn't have to pursue... she *was* pursued. Period. When she wanted to be seen with someone, she wanted to be seen with the elite. The most fly young nigga in the neighborhood. One of the AMG boys. They were called that because they had 3 sets C, E, and S. If you didn't own your own trap, you couldn't be an E, but Bolo was a C Class that moved and felt like an E. Plus, he spoke almost exclusively in slang. That rebel gangsta talk was a turn-on sometimes.

But times change. Little girls grow up. Guys that are named after cars don't. Seeing her man at the trap with all the thugs was so exciting at first, but the excitement vanished once it was time to live like adults. She was living with her mother and brother. She tried to get Bolo to come to college with her. Yeah right. He barely even called her his girl anymore. He didn't even call her Sienna, just shawty. It was cute at first, but it started to replace her name. She watched him go to jail once for 3 months, but she didn't sweat it That was "a part of this street shit," he would tell her. She was ready to ride with him and hold it down. She could pick the money up from the spot and put it on his books. Hell, she could sell the dope if she had to. Why not? She's good at math. She's been around the life. She figured she could do it if she had to.

It wasn't until he was in for a few weeks that things started to change. Everyone was saying "Free Bolo" as if his being in jail was someone else's fault or some grave injustice. He knew what he was doing would land him in jail eventually. He told her that all the time. She started to realize it was just something people said to fit in. It really meant nothing. No problem. He's got his gang. The AMG was going to lookout for one of their own. Hell, she'd be protected, too; after three weeks or so, reality set in. She reached out to his friends to get more money for his books. Nothing. She went to the trap, and they treated her like some street walking hoe. She even tried to buy some dope to sell... they didn't even respect her or take her seriously. No matter what she did, all they wanted was some pussy. It was like a competition to see who could fuck Bolo's girl while he was away. She wasn't the trap queen she thought she was. She was just alone. That's when the other girls started popping up. She knew Bolo had hoes, but the depth of his relationship with them and the sheer numbers made her sick to her stomach. It felt like he was balancing 10 different women, and she wasn't any more special than the rest of them. The difference was that they knew about her. She didn't know about them. Not by name. Now she did. They would call and message to ask how he was doing. He even dared to ask her to reach out to them for whatever reasons he thought of at the time.

By the time Bolo was out, Sienna had been hit with a reality check. She'd played herself. Instead of developing herself to be independent and finding a man developing himself for the same thing, she spent her time chasing a polished worker bee pretending to be rich, pretending to be successful, pretending to give a damn about her. He pretended to be who she thought he was. The worst part was that he didn't choose her. She chose him! She hadn't respected herself enough not to be bought off by new shoes and gold teeth. Now her peers were off to college, or the military, or getting their careers started, and she was running around looking dumb and broke. She thought she was looking down on everyone else before, but now the world was looking down on her.

Bolo didn't change when he came home. He was twenty-three, doing all the same shit he'd been doing the whole time. Ratchet women, looser homeboys glorifying Jordans and Cars. Everything was about "the streets." Everything was a scheme, a lick, a move, a crime... a disgrace. She wasn't even proud to be his anymore. She wasn't proud of herself, and that made her violent. A bitch in the trap? She's fighting. A bitch dance on him at the club? She's fighting. She'd slap a bitch for even looking at her the wrong way. She'd claim it was disrespect, but the truth was that she felt like people could sense the failure she'd let herself become. She thought they could see it, and she would do anything to make them stop looking.

She wasn't the only one that had gotten more violent. Life was catching up with Bolo too. The intimidation and respect he once exerted on his peers was waning. His desperate grabs for power started manifesting themselves in fistfights and even shootings. All the "have nots" were getting jobs and starting a business. All the "lames" were starting to get educated, get jobs, find partners. They became preoccupied with their own pursuits of happiness, and the things Bolo found important were little more than novelties to them now. He'd began to hate them for that, and he'd take that hate out on rival gang members. Even his own friends had become dangerous, shooting at each other over nothing. His world had become one of anger and depression, and all the pills and weed and alcohol couldn't heal what he felt was broken.

Sienna could see it coming before he slapped her for the first time. Money was low. Bolo was at the trap trying to break down some zips, and he needed some bags and some batteries for the scale. Sienna went to the store, but they were out, and Hobby Lobby was closed. When she got to the trap, all she could get was some trash bags from her house. Yeah, that should work. When she explained what happened, she could feel the air get thick and all the eyes of his "friends" on her. She had embarrassed him, and now he would embarrass her. She can hardly remember exactly what he said; all she heard was "Bitch," and she felt the sting of his slap. Her world went bright white, and as she was falling to the ground, she watched him walk away and say, "Bruh, these hoes ain't shit for real." And her heart broke.

That was her thanks. That's what she got for being his girlfriend. That's what she got for looking down her nose to everyone else thinking she was elite. She wasn't elite; she was on the floor of the trap. She'd hit rock bottom. She could tell Rico. Bolo had a sort of respect for Rico. "I fuck with your brother. He cool. I wouldn't say he no pussy or nothing like that he can come around but he doing what he do I'm doing what I do," he'd told her once before. The problem was that if Rico found out there would be blood, she couldn't guarantee it would be Bolo's blood. Bolo could be vicious but so could Rico. It's been a few months now, and he'd slapped her around twice more since then. It was way past time to go.

"... You feel me."

"Yeah, I understand, Bolo" She'd hardly been paying attention. She wanted to tell him how much she hated him now. The truth was that she only half hated him. She jumped into this thinking she was taking advantage of the situation; more than that, he was just as disillusioned with his dope boy dreams as she was. He would never admit it, but she started to feel like Bolo was running on autopilot. He was a victim of his upbringing, and she couldn't help but pity the lost little boy pretending to be important while surrounding himself with dropouts and crack heads. He was still a big dog in his world, but his world had been reduced to a hand full of neighborhoods surrounding Lincoln Way. Where was the sexy street nigga that would command respect in public and be her personal confidant in private? Those days were so long gone that they didn't even feel as if they'd ever happened. What did a high school girl really know about respect anyway?

Here they were in the car driving back from his PO's office. She always had to drive him because they'd taken his license. Apparently, being from the AMG didn't mean shit in the real world. His phone rang, and she instinctively looked at the screen. Monica flashed across it. He picked it up and made a pitiful attempt at making a booty call sound like a business transaction. She doesn't even know why she bothered to say anything, but she did, which led to his "Devotion and loyalty" speech again. She was so tired of hearing about the necessary evils of being with a street nigga. She said she'd understood, and that seemed to satisfy him for now.

"Don't even trip. Run me to DJ crib real quick. I need to pick up some money. Once I grab that, Imma throw you something to get your hair done and grab some food and shit. Tomorrow we going to that Gucci Mane show, so grab me some shoes and make sure your nails match my shit. If you look crazy, you ain't going."

"Lucky me," she thought sarcastically. "Thanks, Bae," she said.

They pulled up to DJ's house, and Bolo hopped out of the car. "Go to the QT and grab me some blunt wraps and get some gas if you need it," he said, handing her a $20. She pulled off as he stepped inside. Sienna parked the car at the hair store across the gas station. Bolo always liked to park where he couldn't be seen, and he always backed in. Sienna had picked up on that habit and adopted it. She didn't need gas, so there was no need to clog the pumps. Sienna hated going to the QT by herself because there were always guys just hanging around. She wondered why they didn't go back to whatever life they had. Did they even have lives? They'd always stare, and every now and then, one of them would muster the courage to say something to her. It was usually something rude that was meant to be polite. If she responded with something they didn't like, they'd respond in kind. By now, she'd learned not to make eye contact and just pretend she didn't see them.

The line was four people long, and the guy in front of her was talking on the phone in a way that made it clear he thought he was being quiet.

"Aight bet, so what you trying to do? Don't be acting scared and shit nigga. Stall him out till I get there. Did you see who was with him? Oh, he got dropped off. Bet."

That got her attention. Was he talking about her? Bolo? She looked at how he was dressed. Camo jacket, jeans, slightly used Jordans looked like they had been cleaned in a sink with a toothbrush. She looked out in the parking lot and saw a dodge charger with tinted windows. All signs of the illustrious "street nigga."

"Get on the game with that nigga or som'. Give me bout 10 mins Imma come in through the bag."

No question now. DJ had a busted window in his house with a bag where the outside screen should be. If he let the glass up in the house, the only thing there was a plastic bag. This was a set-up. They were going to rob Bolo or worse.

Sienna's blood ran cold. She wanted to run, but something inside her told her to stay calm and think. Bolo had become a piece of shit, but he didn't deserve to die. Before she could think about what she was doing, she was walking back to her car, struggling to look nonchalant. As she rode back to DJ's crib, she thought of a plan. She tried to call Bolo, but his phone kept sending her voice mail. He'd probably turned it off after the Monica incident. Sienna was too afraid to walk in the front door because now she knew DJ was in on *it*. There was only one way in the house that she could think 0f. The "bag" window. It'd only been 5 ruins since she'd left the gas station and Mr. Camo Coat was likely still in line, having underestimated the speed of his purchase. Sienna parked two doors down at an abandoned house and moved through the back yards to not be seen.

She hugged the house and saw the bag window puffed out, meaning the interior window was open. She knew the bag window was in the rear. What she didn't know was if DJ and Bolo were alone. She raised one shaky hand and lifted the black bag. As she approached the window, she could hear Bob and DJ playing a video game and smell weed smoke in the air. Thank God the music was loud enough to drown out any noise she was making. Confident the room was empty, she climbed through the window. She saw this was a bedroom, maybe a guest room, when she looked around. The room had a small bed, A TV, an aged wooden nightstand with a phone charger, a few pens, some change, and discarded cigar tobacco hastily dumped in ashtrays.

"Ok, now I'm here," Sienna thought. Her mind racing with the grim possibility of dying in this place. She hadn't even realized in her rush to get here she hadn't formulated a plan. Should she hide in the closet? Should she run out and warn Bolo? Should she come to her senses and get the fuck out of there?

"Damn."

She heard outside the window she'd just come out of. Time was running out. What would happen if the would-be killer caught her? Would he attack her? She began to panic, then it hit her. He doesn't know who you are. She said a quick prayer and stuck her head out the window. When her eyes met Mr. Camo Coat's, the world stopped. He looked like someone that wouldn't hesitate to kill her. She couldn't help but wonder how someone with eyes so cold and a face so rough could walk around society without immediately raising the suspicions of everyone they met. Who was his mother? Better yet, who was fucking him? Yeesh. She steeled herself enough to speak.

"Aye, he said come this way, hurry up," she said, trying to sound as controlled as she could.

Camo Coat paused and grabbed his waist, reaching for his gun. He paused as if considering what she had said and how many shots to dump into her face. His expression softened, then he spoke.

"Aight, Bet. Watch out."

Of course. She was in the window. How was he supposed to fit? Sienna backed into the room and crouched down. As Camo climbed through the window, he saw something flash before his eyes. It was such an instant he couldn't react. He just paused; half crouched in a window frame. He felt what seemed like a feather tickling the tip of his nose ... then his chin. As he reached up to touch his face, he felt what felt like a hard stick protruding from where he'd just lost sight. Then came an unnatural burning feeling on his face. By the time he realized he'd been stabbed, there was another flash. He would never know what he'd seen or felt.

Sienna was now in full panic. She was pinned under a twitching 200 lb. man with two ink pens protruding from his bleeding eye sockets, waiting for someone to walk in and kill her. After five of the longest seconds of her life, she realized no one had heard. She relaxed and allowed Camo to lie on top of her, giving him a sort of lovers' embrace. She slid him to the side to crawl from under him. As his blood began to trickle on her, she couldn't help but feel a dark intimacy in being the only witness and provider of this man's end.

Bloom-boom.

Sienna didn't have any experiences with heart failure or heart attacks, but she knew if she could drop dead from shock, she would have done it at that moment. Camo's gun had fallen out of his pants onto the wooden floor. Now she could hear two sets of footsteps and a gun cock. She was about to be found out, and whoever opened that door was going to start shooting. She reached for the gun.

She grabbed the revolver on the floor and squeezed the trigger three times as the door opened. There was the sound of bodies dropping as she scrambled to her feet. Bolo was lifting himself off of DJ and spun to face her. His eyes bulged at the sight of Sienna.

"What the fuck?!"

"It was a set-up! They were trying to kill you," she said in a whimper that was meant to be a scream. It was then that she felt hot tears running down her face. She was so terrified that she was almost numb. At this point, nothing mattered anymore. If Camo hopped up, it didn't matter. If DJ jumped up and killed her, it'd be ok. She had let go of any idea of self-preservation and had resigned herself to whatever fate was meant for her. She sat there crying for a moment. When her vision cleared, Bolo grabbed her.

"Damn, give it to me."

"Huh"

"Give me the gun. Where did you park?"

"Across the street, I didn't ..."

"Just hold up, damn. Fuck you think they set me up for?"

"I heard him at the gas station saying he was coming and you were here, and I didn't know what to do. I tried to warn you and you didn't answer your phone, so I snuck in, and he came behind me, and I grabbed a pen, and then his gun fell and—" Sienna said in one long run-on.

"Aight aight damn, shit, aight."

Sienna noticed that Bolo was grabbing his shoulder. He'd been hit. He took the gun from Sienna and shot it into an already dead DJ.

"12 going to be here in a minute; you need to go home, bleach your shit and throw the whole outfit away. It's some money in the living room; grab it and go. You got bout 30 seconds."

Sienna was on her feet before she knew it. She had pocketed what felt like $500 in mixed bills.

"Let's go," she said, looking at a pale-faced Bolo.

"I can't go with you. You can't take me to the hospital. They gon say buddy tried to rob us, and we all got fucked up in the mix. Go."

Sienna ran to climb out the window, only looking back once.

"I love you," she said, meaning it for the first time in a long time.

"I already know, now gon."

seven
can't knock the hustle

THERE'S something inherently urban about flying in the face of traditional fashion standards. They say the clothes make the man. A sharp suit can make even the most meager man feel like a king. A suit is just an event-appropriate outfit that signifies how well prepared the wearer is for the given situation. In Lincoln Way, the most common outfit is high-priced athletic wear juxtaposed with elegant jewelry. The average earner in America can't afford to wear designer material, yet they long to wear it. To middle-class America, this doesn't make sense. Why would those with below-average income be so irresponsible as to spend a significant amount of money on premium clothing that serves no real purpose for the most part?

The answer, of course, is the illusion of wealth and success. The struggle of the lower middle class is so common that it's hardly a struggle at all. Poverty is simply a fact of life. Escaping the economic conditions is as realistic to some as winning the lotto: Sure, you've heard about people doing it, but you don't know anyone that has. The odds seem so astronomical that those who are the most vocal about "leaving the hood" face ridicule and contempt. "That nigga think he smart, or something," or other common phrases are passed from one failed attempted ascent to the next, compounding the idea that this is your home. The idea of representing your hood became a twisted idiom that went from "Remember where you've come from" to "Don't think you'll ever leave." Once resigned to that, the journey for personal success becomes a competition. If you're never to leave, how are you to grow? This leads to a dog-eat-dog mentality. Internal competition is born when the dreams of the neighborhood are confined to that neighborhood. It's no longer about winning against oppressive institutions; it becomes about defeating those around you. Your very neighbors become your opposition. One-upmanship becomes a way of life.

This is where the Hustle or Die mentality stems from in Rico's mind.

Once the hood gave up on fighting systemic oppression, they began oppressing each other. Niggas don't want to be rich; they want to be "hood rich." They want the cars and the clothes that no one else in the hood can afford. This gives them an air of superiority. This makes them feel special, at least among the down-trodden. These are the hustlers. They'll do anything to outshine those around them, including committing crimes. The women wanted men who could provide, so they tailored themselves and their mentality to match these hustlers. This gave rise to the killers. Those who cannot do, teach. Those who cannot hustle, kill those who can. It didn't matter how you got your fancy cars or clothes. All that mattered was that the things you had were more exclusive than the things the next person could acquire. How far was a person willing to go to feel elite? The further a man was willing to go gained respect: rob, pimp, sell drugs, kill. Ironically, the lengths a woman was willing to go gained her condemnation: rob, prostitute, sell drugs, kill. The men had enough competition with each other not to want to compete with the women, too. Hence, they created a culture that fostered their peers' power-obsessed and ruthless nature and crippled the same qualities in their partners for fear of betrayal. These are the origins of the rules of the streets. It all comes back to the eternal desire to be fresher than the competition.

Rico spent his entire life watching these competitions play out. A part of him wondered is this what genuine success felt like. Being inducted into the CABAL felt like he'd cheated the system in a way he couldn't quite explain.

It'd been 2 weeks since his tenure as assistant manager of the club.

His duties were minimal: greet guests, maintain manpower, anticipate logistical needs, and observe. Those were the instructions Mr. Prescott gave him before handing him off to Money Mike, the head of the CABAL Lounge and one of Mr. Prescott's inner circle.

"Aight, check it out we got three sections filled, we on a roll, we getting money now baby, what you got in that bag?" Mike was going over the reservations for the upcoming Luke James show.

Rico liked Mike. They had a sort of "odd couple" relationship. Mike was older, but he respected Rico's intelligence and ability to adapt. Rico respected Mike for the same reasons and his cool head. Mike was flashy in a way Rico wasn't, but Rico appreciated Mike's taste. Mike was a hustler born and bred. For Mike, money was the name of the game. Mike came from Lansing, 1\11 Rico asked why he didn't go back to visit more often a few times. Mike would respond, "Ain't nothing out there for real just hard times and slow money unless you know folks ... then it's hard times and fast money. I ain't with all the hard times, though." He'd say with a slight laugh. Mr. Prescott had told Rico that Mike was a hustler's hustler. He'd found him by looking for him in an unusual way. Mike's name was all over town for his ability to supply weed to the weed suppliers, but he was rarely seen in the trap spots for more than 10 minutes. He moved like someone with a social reputation to uphold because he did. Mike was class Valedictorian of St. Maria University; he was a junior league basketball coach.

At 6'2, husky and dark-complected, He was an intimidating-looking character, and he knew it, so he'd spent a lot of time finding ways to make sure people around him found him approachable. Especially white people. Mike would buy the things the hood loved, like his Jet Black Lexus or his fully customized Challenger. He'd drive the Lexus when handling business and the Challenger to less reputable certain events. Mike believed in power through compartmentalization. He believed that there was a certain way to do things and a certain place for everything, especially when dealing. If done right, there was no need for underhanded tactics. He believed that he could stay in power because of his strong moral standings. Mike would give his son $200 to buy new shoes then instruct him to give the change to a homeless person. "You see, son, we were blessed to know how to hustle. We can't be selfish with that. As long as we're eating, we can't be afraid to feed others because if they starve, they may want to eat us, and then everybody loses." Mike controlled three neighborhoods in the city; he was admired by the thugs, the dealers, and accepted by whites. Money Mike was a Multifaceted Hustler.

"Just a hoodie I grabbed on the way in. Three tables already? At this rate, every section will be sold out by Wednesday. That might be a problem because some people will want to show up with a lot of cash and no questions. What are we going to do about them? Turn them away and fuck up our reputation?" Rico said, concerned.

"I ain't worried about that. The streets have their own shit. See niggas send they workers in here to run the floors and fuck with the lil' bougie hoes and shit. I always leave three table sections for anybody that's getting money and wanna pull up and have a good time. It's like a reward. If you are in my territory and you are on your shit and coming back with your numbers right, you can come with me to the CABAL and play. If I'm running shit, I'm trying to mix and mingle with other people that are running shit too. That's why we have the Booths." He said, pointing up to the skybox section.

"When Mr. P put me together here, he let me run this muthafucka the way I saw fit. I already had the ear of the streets, and my Alumni contacts put me close to the banks, firms, and shit like that. Coaching my son's football team got my face good with the suburbs. A few golf games later, white folks want to rent booths and shit. It's a status symbol. They don't come. But their college-age kids do. That's the future of the legit money around here. So, what do I do? I stagger them out. Every even-numbered box is legit money; every odd number is street money. This way, they can deal with each other, and it's all under my watch, so they all have to deal with me. The white folks have an incentive to preserve black neighborhoods, and the gangsters have an incentive to keep the violence down. Anybody fuck up the situation they get cast out."

"Damn, that's smart, so which section do you fit in? Which is yours?" Rico asked slyly, challenging Mike's belief in whether he considered himself a legitimate business or a street king.

Mike laughed. "All of them."

Rico laughed at Mike's cleverness. It'd been a busy week. There were promotions and advertisements all over the place for the Cardi B showcase, and there were more than a few rumors of a guest appearance from the Migos. It felt like everyone with a membership to the Lounge would be there. Rico knew the fire marshal would be in full effect, but Mike told him not to sweat it. They would make sure not to violate. Rico and Mike went over their plans and positioning for bartenders, security, maintenance, and DJs. They were preparing for a big-time guest, and things seemed to be moving well. As Rico left the meeting, he couldn't help but wonder what Mr. Prescott had in mind for his future. Rico seemed to be doing well with the club, and people seemed to accept his presence there, thanks to Money Mike. Rico was ready to go, so he grabbed his bag and made his exit. On his way out, he pressed a button on the staff elevator.

"Can you bring the car around?"

Rico imagined having a loft in the CABAL, but was much more comfortable in Lincoln Way. He would split his time between the two places. Most times, he'd prepare to catch the bus, but lately, he's gotten used to being driven.

Once he left the elevator of the subterranean parking deck, he was greeted by the white Range Rover he'd coveted. With Prescott out of town, Adonis was assigned to be Rico's driver and right-hand man.

"Sup Don."

"Oh... what's up." Adonis always spoke as if he didn't expect to be a part of a conversation. His calm demeanor didn't reflect his size. Adonis didn't really talk...to anybody. Adonis was a good name for the 6′3 former athlete. Rico didn't know much about Adonis, except he was from Miami and used to play Semi-Pro football until a career-ending injury derailed his gridiron dreams. Rico felt lucky to know that much.

"Let me ask you something: What made you want to do this? Why are you working for the CABAL?" Rico asked as they began to ride.

"Money," Adonis said with what sounded like a hint of a chuckle. Rico checked the mirror. No trace of a smile.

"Look, man, I don't know how Mr. P does things, but I like to get to know the people around me. That's how you build a team and relationships. I mean, how long can you keep this robot shit up?" Rico said, half-joking.

"I'm just doing my job, man. What do you want me to do to start a conversation? Pretend that we're friends? I don't have a problem with you or anything; I just don't have anything I wanna talk about."

Rico thought for a moment. "Ok, how about this. Who's your favorite football team?"

"I don't follow teams, only players."

Rico stared at him through the rearview. He was careful not to express himself; he just looked at him, leaving maximum room to talk.

"Dolphins."

"You're a Lil Wayne fan too. I figured. I figured something else out too ..."

"What makes you say that?" Adonis asks, briefly glancing at the rearview.

"Well, it was hardly noticeable at first, but when I first started riding with you, I could see the track displays even with the volume muted. I'm a big rap fan too. Being a Wayne fan, tells me you're into the words and not just the beat. Wayne's basically the 2nd best rapper alive."

Rico let it hang in the air. He figured he'd extended the olive branch enough to make it clear it was there. From here, the ball was in Adonis' court to decide whether or not he was game or not. The silence lingered for what felt like 2 minutes.

"Let me guess you're a Jay-Z fan."

Rico shrugged his shoulders.

Adonis spoke again. "Jay's cool. I figured you were more into the drill and stuff like that if anything," Adonis said with an audible eye roll.

"Really, what about me made you think that?" Rico challenged.

Adonis paused, thinking and relaxed. "My bad, man, maybe I read you wrong. I'm used to seeing guys thirsty to be around the Club or the studio. At this point, I just expect it."

Rico was slightly offended, but something about the annoyance in his voice. The lack of tolerance for the bullshit that came with the CABAL's prestige made Rico comfortable. In a world that revolves around glitz, glamor, money, and lies, Adonis prefers to keep silent. Rico figured that was his way of staying focused and grounded. Rico was starting to like Adonis. He seemed like someone that he'd want to keep close to him. He wondered if Prescott thought the same thing. Was that why he hired him, or was there another reason?

"We're here."

Rico stepped out of the car and took a look at his home in Lincoln Way. The contrast between his rather homely neighborhood and the CABAL never seemed so obvious as it had lately. "Aight, Don see you tomorrow. When we have events at the lounge, I want you to come in and stick by my side. Ya know, to watch my back in the club. I'm still new; ya feel me."

"Are you sure Mr. P is good with that?" Adonis asked as straight-faced as ever.

"Yeah, he said you're my driver; just think of it as driving me: getting me around the club same as you'd do in a car."

"Alright ..." Adonis said, concerned, "Rico, You're forgetting your bag."

"No, I'm not, that's you," Rico said as he walked towards the unimpressive small house.

Adonis looked in the bag and saw a Green and Orange XL hoodie with a Miami Dolphins logo across the front. Rico never looked back to confirm it; but he was sure he heard the crack of a smile.

eight
options

RICO WAS NEVER much for going to the club. He found the whole experience to be somewhat abrasive. It wasn't that he didn't like music or that he couldn't dance; he just didn't enjoy how public and unpredictable the environment was. Sure, he'd gone out with Alanna and even Monica a few times back in the day, but it was rare he went out now. He didn't like the idea that some of his peers lived their lives from Saturday to Saturday to go out and spend money on overpriced drinks. Those who embraced these pointless routines were always at home in places where it was easy to be fought or shot at over a minor disagreement. For most people, the club is a masquerade: be who you wish you were and try to convince everyone that's who you really are all the time. Rico also didn't like the way time melted away when clubbing. It always felt like everyone was there waiting for something magical to happen. It was a ceremony of sorts: a tribal dance to bring blessings of love and adoration from strangers looking to bring the same things to themselves. For Rico, the club always felt like Mardi Gras without the soul. As he was able to look around the CABAL during one of its most profitable nights of the year, the place felt like Sodom and Gomorrah and Rico struggled not to get swept up in the hedonistic decadence.

"I heard you got everything looking right Rico. How'd you get those last hundred bottles of D'usse at the last minute?" Mr. Prescott asked over the phone sounding pleased.

"I have a homeboy named Tim Eaddy. He's a Soldier on Fort Bragg. Big wild joker, but he's sharp as a tack, and he's solid. He said he could get bottles we couldn't access out here on the base and for a cheaper price. After that, it was just a matter of having a bunch of America's finest purchase the whole supply, and we bought the bottles from them. They each made money, and we saved all at the same time. I told Mike about the whole thing, and he loved the idea. Get this he even sent some of the club girls to do the collecting. Just a little incentive so we can call on those guys in the future if we're in a jam."

"Hell yeah, we eating over here, BOY!" Mike yelled into the phone as he passed. Rico had worked the club for a few weeks now, and things had been running smoothly. The learning curve wasn't as steep as he'd thought Running a Nightclub was similar to managing a grocery store or selling dope. Revenue was the name of the game. You had to acquire and maintain relevant personnel. This was easy for the most part because the CABAL had plenty of vetted staff. Rico was unfamiliar with the CABAL's normal recruiting practices; all he knew was that you were not to be questioned once you were in. Each staff member has a private story, and that was fine. Rico always knew where and when to pry. All that mattered to him, for the time being, was the fact that he'd never seen a more professional staff in his whole life. He was sure the money was good, but the adulation kept everyone in top shape. They didn't just work there. They took real pride in their work.

Supply maintenance and logistics was about keeping logs of what was needed versus what they had in stock. Consumables were supplies that would disappear like food, drinks, toiletries, glasses. In the case of the CABAL, they also needed to have "special consumables" such as celebrity guests, call girls (or boys) for their guests' particular taste, live bands, and dancers were regular but consistently replaceable, expenses that were necessary for the lounge to function.

Accommodation and Maintenance were all about keeping the CABAL on the cutting edge of entertainment. Long-term investments like the skybox's furniture and consistent updates on the structure and visual appeal of the place were typically high cost but low-frequency expenses. Keeping the power, plumbing, and kitchen equipment rolling were low-cost, high frequency expenses since that had to be maintained every month.

The overhead was the cost of supporting all of these moving parts. Everything from the payroll, marketing, lawyer retainers, accountants, and buildings security systems were all covered in overhead. If it costs money regularly, it was the overhead. Rico knew that the goal of the business was to make enough money to exceed the overhead as much as possible. If your business costs two thousand dollars, you need to regularly make three or four thousand to stay afloat.

The CABAL wasn't about staying afloat; the CABAL was about profit The most important thing in business. After all the expenses and overhead, the profit makes it all worth it. Profit is what allows a person to live in comfort. Profit feeds power, and the more of each you have, the more the other will be attracted to you. Profit changes life for the good and the bad.

"How long are you going to be out of town? We're just trying to hold things down until you get back." Rico asked humbly.

"Doesn't sound like you're having a hard time to me. Mike knows the ropes and could probably run the whole CABAL if he wasn't so obsessed with being in control of the women and flash. That's why I put him in charge. This is his arena. In the lounge, he's a king, and the people love him. He obviously respects you because he kicks them to the curb every time I send him someone to work with. He calls you "Cuz" when he talks about you. That kind of respect can't be bought or stolen, only earned."

Given a chance, Prescott always had a lesson ready to fire off in the holster. Rico was starting to get used to it.

"So, I'm guessing my father respected you?" Rico had a gun of his own.

"Look, we'll talk about that when I get back in town. I know you have questions, and I want to sit down face to face with you and get through all the answers. I called you to get the Blue Key from Mike at the end of the night. He has it and knows what to do with it. Look, I gotta go. I'll holla at you in a few days. Hold it down and don't forget that Blue Key."

"Blue Key, 'right I got you no doubt." Rico always felt certain anxiety when he saw Mr. Prescott's name on his phone. He was always hanging on his every word, trying to find some sort of meaning. He was always learning, but he felt like he was being fed knowledge without information. "The time will come," he told himself.

"Rico, one of the girls upstairs, is requesting an autograph from Luke." Adonis, for his stature, could be quite stealthy.

"No problem; when he gets off stage, have someone walk him through the Skybox. Let him know we'll cover any autograph fees but make sure we have pictures taken in ways that show off the establishment and only have him autograph pamphlets that say "CABAL" so people will associate the celebrity encounter with us."

"Ok cool" Adonis looks up toward the skyboxes and smoothed his eyebrow to indicate to the concierge that everything is a "go."

"I thought I told you to have a good time? You can't do that unless you smile or something. People are already curious about the new assistant manager. With you around, they're going to think you're my security."

"I kinda am," Adonis said with a dry sense of humor.

"Who would want to hurt you? Not that it matters I'll protect you," a catlike voice emerged from thin air to Rico's surprise. The sound of poison champagne. Arrogance and lust and cunning wrapped in rose petals.

"This doesn't look like any rehab I've ever seen," Rico said unamused.

"Well, sometimes you need to rehabilitate from rehabilitation. Besides, it was boring. I only went because of that trifling ass judge." Alanna said with a feigned grimace.

She was always too good looking for her own good. Honey brown skin, hanging curls, long lashes, and lips that probably supplied Christmas bonus money every year to the workers at Maybelline. She stood there in a Red and Black cocktail dress and Black heels that made her slightly taller than Rico.

The dress looked easy enough to get into, but she'd most likely laugh at you for trying.

Rico spoke, "I didn't know you were back."

"Oh really? Well, I heard all about you and your new position. I just had to show a little leg and find my way up in here to see. I'm not surprised you're here. It fits you. You lowkey boogie anyway." She mused, giving an amused look and sipping from her glass.

Rico recognized the glass from the Sky lounge. He looked up, wondering who'd brought her.

"I'm here with PJ." She'd followed Rico's gaze. "You can get anywhere you want if you show a little interest in the uninteresting."

"I guess the judge wasn't impressed," Rico said, making direct eye contact.

"Oh, don't look at me so serious; you know it makes me weak," she responded, deflecting his verbal jab. "Besides, why do you care? Would you rather me be here with you? You might convince me..."

"You know what's gonna happen if PJ thinks a girl with his crew left with someone else?"

"Don't worry, you've got a big bodyguard," She quipped.

"But you don't.nYou're playing with the wrong people," Rico snapped. PJ ran cocaine on the Westside, and he was Money Mike's half-brother. He was a felon that never quite readjusted to his life in freedom. Rico had met him a few times, and there was respect there, but not much else. Rico knew that PJ looked at the most woman as accessories for his outfits when he went out. He didn't get emotionally invested, but he would throw a chick out of a moving car if she disrespected him and think nothing of it.

"That's your problem. Stop trying to save me. I'm not going to let anything happen to me. PJ just better be happy I let him be seen with me. Don't you think I should be seen?" She asked sarcastically while stroking Rico's chin. Alanna loved to play with him. They'd dated on and off, but she was a wild card. She was broke as everyone else in Lincoln Way, but she knew how to manipulate people using her looks. She wasn't known to sleep around, but Rico had his suspicions. He grabbed her hand.

"Glad you're out. Just stay out of trouble."

"I'm not worried, but if you get in any trouble, call me ..." She said, walking away, "..and tell Sienna I said hi."

Rico watched as she walked away. As soon as things got serious, she asked him to marry her. Two weeks later, she disappeared. When she returned, she was in trouble for drunk driving. After that, it was court and rehab. A whirlwind romance that amounted to little more than a fling between two on-again and off-again lovers. Rico stuck his hand in his pocket to find a napkin with a phone number on it. Alanna's number.

"Um ... what happened there," Adonis asked, amused.

"Shiid look like Rico been busting moves and ain't telling nobody."

Money Mike chimed in on cue as he approached. "I ain't mad that Lil bitch kinda fine. I knew something was up when she came in with bruh and them. Bruh has hoes, but she looks a little put together to be riding with them."

"Think it'll be a problem," Adonis asked, making eye contact with Mike.

"Nah, you can take all that air out ya chest big dog. That nigga probably doesn't even realize she came downstairs. This nigga Luke singing got all these hoes' attention in this muthafucka anyway. Of course, you know I found something for me to fuck on later, after we count this money," Mike always gleamed when it came to counting the money. He *always* had enough time to count the money no matter how late it got.

Rico changed the subject "Aye Mike, I just got off the phone with Prescott. He said something about you getting a Blue key."

"Oh, ok, I know what he talking about. I got it. Link up with me after shit slows down. Try not to get caught up in these hoes. I see you over there, Boy!" he suddenly yelled over Rico's shoulder at Dillon "Mac Truck" Mac, an up-and-coming Heisman trophy candidate dancing with some brown haired model.

The CABAL was jumping as expected. The people were engaged by the decadence and modern sensibility of the place. Even Rico felt like a prince in a kingdom of designer clothes and expensive cognac. Luke James was in rare form, breaking into his hit single "Options," which caused the whole event to stop and take notice. The passionate conflicting lyrics were at the same time masculine and vulnerable in a way that so few artists know how to convey. He was an unassuming sort of talent. He wasn't flashy and didn't surf on movie-star looks.

He looked like a regular relatable person with an unfair amount of talent. Rico knew that talent is only revealed through hard work, so he respected artists who fine-tuned their craft while remaining humble.

"It's hard to make a love song from a man's perspective that doesn't sound soft. This joint isn't really for the ladies; it sounds to me like it's giving a voice to the fellas," Rico mused aloud.

"I see you're a fan like me," Adonis acknowledged. "Wait till it builds up." Midway through the song, the lights dimmed and from the crowd on the middle dance floor emerged rapper Rick Ross performing his guest verse on the track draped in designer brands Rico wouldn't even know where to find. "That's that 305 right there," Adonis beamed with pride while not changing his ever-present straight man expression.

Rico didn't respond. He'd been a fan of Rick Ross for years. He often considered him one of the most underrated lyricists and found his street savvy and sophisticated music relatable and inspiring. This type of music made places like the CABAL shine the brightest. This was music that understood.

The night had proved to be a memorable one. This was the biggest event Rico had helped manage at the CABAL, and things had gone perfectly. As the night wound to a close, Rico said his goodbyes to the staff, and Mike walked up looking like he swam in the money instead of counting it.

"We getting money out here B. You ready to get this key or what?" "Yeah, I'm cool; let's go," Rico responded, satisfied with the nights events.

They headed into Mike's office. This was Rico's first time inside. The place was black and white with red accents. The two largest pictures on the wall were Ice Cube and Michael Jordan. There was also a bachelor's degree on the wall from Talladega College.

"You gotta let'em know we ain't no dummies out here," Mike said, watching Rico's eyes.

Mike pulled out a small blue box and handed it to Rico. As Rico grabbed the box, Mike held firm and gave him a brief but intense look.

"We don't prick fingers around here. We lock-in and win. Period. You feel me?"

"I got you," Rico said, sobered by the intensity of the moment. "What is this a Key to?"

"Shit, your future for real, but if you want to be technical, it's a penthouse here in the building. You going on the books now. Shit real now. You got ya Lil stripes showing you can handle business. Don't start thinking you "Big Meech" or nothing, but you graduated from peon to a nigga whose name I remember," Mike said laughing. "You just gotta know that this is like a welcoming party. You're being given a chance to lock-in. Your foot is in the door. There's still a lot of shit you gotta do to make it in this world."

"Who do you want me to shoot," Rico said, laughing.

"Why, can you shoot?" Mike said with a cold dead stare.

Rico understood. He wasn't being asked to shoot anyone, but such a request wasn't off the table.

"Ok, before I take this. Who ran shit before Mr. Prescott?"

"I don't know for real. Some OG nigga that got ghost. I know you trying to find out about your dad and shit, but bruh, if I knew, I'd tell you. I can tell you that the higher you are up on the food chain, the more information you have access to. I'm at the point where I can do what I want, when I want, where I want, as long as it makes sense. You can get there; you just gotta be on point. I got ears everywhere. I know you used to bust your lil moves and shit out in the streets before you started doing the 9 to 5, but now you are about to be playing with real money. Street hustling was the way for me. You were making 2-300? I was making 70-80 thousand. That was my way in. I can tell you now your way in is by using that head. You smart and niggas can tell you'll take it there if it comes down to some street shit that's why niggas fuck with you. Depend on that and you'll be good. From this point on, I'm fucking with you."

Money Mike's words hit home. Rico treated his time at the CABAL as a side hustle even though it took up most of his time. He made more than he could have dreamed at Food Shark, but he wouldn't be buying any Mercedes any time soon. Now it seems everything that's happened so far had been an introduction ... an initiation of sorts. Now he had started to build relationships without even really trying. Adonis was starting to become his right-hand man since he requested that he be ever-present. Mr. Prescott didn't have a problem with that. Mike was connected. He knew everybody, and now after spending so much time with Rico, it seemed he also had his back. Rico couldn't help but wonder if this was his own doing or if things were somehow being orchestrated. Now wasn't the time, though. He had a key to the penthouse. The key was just a plastic card, but it represented access. It was a step closer to finding out about his dad. It was a step closer to a new life.

So much for food, shark.

nine
teflon don

J. Lester was a man that knew what he wanted out of life. He wanted to sit at the table with his friends and run his business deals over golf games and horse races. He was a big-time attorney that believed that he deserved to be in the seat of power. He came from a long line of southern aristocrats and was proud of his lineage from the civil war. He believed in the law of the land: whoever owns the land makes the law. He owned plenty of lands. As much as the Mexicans could work. Was he racist? No, racism was for poor people so obsessed with football and beating their wives they could never take some time go to college and get out of the trailer park. He didn't care what happened in the world of minorities. He saw blacks at his place of business, and they were a big help getting his files in order. As a matter of fact, he liked to refer to them as "the help." It was a compliment coming from him. He couldn't quite figure out why they were always so upset about police brutality. Obey the law, and you have nothing to worry about. He didn't look at Native Americans as having been victimized. They were simply conquered people. He came from a line of conquerors. Could he be faulted for that? Of course not.

When Jay was a boy, he and his dad would sit on the porch, drink lemonade and watch the Latinos (that's what they liked to be called) cut the grass and make things look right. His dad would smoke a hand-rolled cigar and tell him that if he didn't work hard and use his head, they would be the ones on the porch, and he'd be the one in the yard. He couldn't imagine a white man of his pedigree doing something like that. Men of his ilk were meant to rule this world one generation at a time. They were pure-blooded leaders. His dad was one. His son would be one. Lately, it seemed like outsiders were starting to crop up more and more in his place of business, calling themselves his equal. His competition. He knew better than that, so he decided to surround himself with men like him. Each year they redrew the school zones so their kids could be surrounded by better, pure children like he was growing up. None of that wild savagery he read about in the inner city news. He donated money to help out those officers of the law that may have shot one of the "others" by mistake in his line of duty. The media didn't seem to understand that those people glorify violence. You'd think they'd be used to being shot and such. He put his time and resources toward keeping the pure from the corrupt. Cleo (Sienna) believes he would have liked her. She was in his wine cellar preparing to do the same thing.

The order came as it always does. Mr. P told her who to keep tabs on and why. She already knew about the GOB. The "good old boys," a right wing radical group that worked to control the city in a way that favored white supremacy by manipulating real estate. They'd buy it from you if you had property at half the value. If you refused, you'd be hearing from the Tax examiner, health inspector, or fire marshal soon enough. If you were just squeaky clean and airtight, well, that was nothing a little arson wouldn't fix. The CABAL was a big fish that was pretty well protected, but its patrons weren't. Floyd's was a barbershop on the east side. It started as a small business. Soon Aubry's BBQ and Breanna's Beans Coffee House helped turn out some of the best businesses in the downtown shopping district. Lester and his GOB couldn't compete, and they couldn't convince any of them to sell the property. When Brianna's nephew Tre was falsely accused of robbery and the local police "accidentally" fired rounds into Sean and Brianna's wedding reception, it was clear the GOB wasn't going away. Cleo was happy she got the call.

Mr. P had managed to get Cleo hired on at the property under a fake name. Lester paid no attention when the head housekeeper informed him there may be a substitute for the next few nights. Now here she was with the perfect plan of execution. As she moved throughout the estate, she did all she could to make sure she wouldn't be identifiable. It's amazing what you can do with some makeup and a hairdo. Cleo knew that she could blend into any environment as a black woman by simply changing her hair. This empire built on a legacy of self-important classism was about to fall as easily as a house of cards because of some yaki. She couldn't help but be amused at the thought. Walking the halls, she could see portraits ofLesters that had come and gone, lived and died in luxury suspended on the backs of overworked and underpaid minorities. Trophy workers shining the shoes and raising the children of these liver-spotted tyrants that attempted to rule from behind lhe shadows. It wouldn't take her long to...

"Ms. Jasmine,"

The voice shook her so hard she nearly yelped in fright. It was one of the grandchildren. Cleo had been in enough of these homes to know that they were all living their Great Gatsby lives of drug abuse, corruption, and excess. Their parents always left housekeepers to help look after them under the guise of working on important business assignments.

"Yes, Master Eric, isn't it past your curfew?" she asked in her most motherly tone.

"Yes, but it's a Saturday, and Pop-Pop said I could do whatever I wanted as long as I didn't leave the main house. I'm good. I just can't go nowhere, according to him."

"Ok, that sounds fun," she said, putting on a fake smile.

"Why don't you turn the light switch? The hallways are dark. I can show you where it is."

Cleo had to think fast. She had to think quickly. She tried to blend seamlessly into the decor and reach her destination without being seen.

"I don't want to disturb your grandfather. He's asleep."

"Ok, that's fine, but I left my backup game controller in the pool house. Do you think you could grab it for me? I don't want to go out there and get yelled at for leaving the house this late. You know the old man will swear I was doing something sneaky."

Eric was an interesting boy. He was a black sheep in the family. He was 16 and had an unpredictable temperament. He was rarely seen with the family since he was caught spending too much time in the pool house with the neighbor Jake. Jacob? Cleo tried not to remember too much about people's backstories. All she knew was that he was gay, and his family resented him for it. He was sent to spend time with his grandfather to see what a "real man" looked like. She wondered what would become of him once the money was his. Would he be a better man than his predecessors, or would he grow to be as arrogant and cruel? The question that hung in the air was should she kill the child.

Hurting children wasn't part of the plan. Even a young man Eric's age was over the line. She hadn't known of him doing anything worthy of a life cut short. She was no saint, but she wasn't evil either.

"Sure, I'll take care of it. Do you need anything else?" she asked, trying not to sound impatient.

"No, not really. Hey..." He thought briefly. "Let me go with you. No one will care if we roll out together. Just leave your apron in the kitchen."

This unexpected request complicated things. Now she was pigeon-holed. The plan was to sneak into the bedroom and cut the old man's throat in his sleep. The plastic knife she brought would melt nicely in the fireplace along with her forged employment records. The whole process wouldn't take five minutes.

"Um ok, sure. Let's go," she said hesitantly. What was his game? She knew it was pretty unusual for someone his age and status to want to move with the help. Cleo dropped the apron as she was told but kept on her latex cleaning gloves. Would she have to hurt the boy?

As they approached the pool house, Eric stopped. They left the rear of the house, and Cleo felt the eyes of nature judging her. The chirps of crickets and the smell of magnolias were oppressive to the senses she used to do her work. Her defenses were failing.

"Can I tell you something? I know you're new here, but you seem chill. You don't seem like the type to rat me out over something stupid."

Not knowing what to say, she replied, "What is it? Is everything ok?"

"Yeah, it's cool. I really wanted to come out here to smoke a J really quickly. You can hit it too if you want; it's no big deal."

Now, this was unexpected. The boy didn't care that she was the help. He didn't even mind sharing his weed with her. Cleo kinda liked this white boy. "I'm ok, but you can go ahead. I won't say anything. We all need a chance to relax and get our minds off things." She responded.

"Thanks. This whole family is bullshit. They always want to act like they know what's up, ya know? Like what's going on in the world, but we're always behind the fence." He said casually, pulling out a sack of weed and some papers.

"What do you mean?" Cleo asked, finding herself genuinely curious.

"I don't know... they're just so old-fashioned about everything. They don't want to change with the times. I don't want to live the old way. I wanna do my own thing. I don't give a fuck about money. I just like normal stuff, not a bunch of stuck-up crap. Tomorrow's my birthday. Of course, the want me to get an expensive watch and... hell, I don't know, bet on some horses or something. I don't want that. I just want to be a part of the world, not above it. You know what I mean?"

"Yeah, but you don't look like you have a bad life," she responded.

"Nah, I know, but... aww crap," they both watched as his rolling paper flew off into the trees outside the property line. "That's my last paper. See what I mean? It's bullshit all the time. I should have put on shoes."

"I got it," Cleo said as she walked toward the wooded area where the joint paper flew.

"Hey, be careful out there; that's not part of the yard. Snakes and poison ivy and all that kinda stuff are out there," He softly yelled at her.

She found the paper about 10 feet into the tree line. As she grabbed it, she noticed the unkempt forest spreading in front of her separating the estates.

"You cool? That was kinda badass how you charged off in the woods like that. That's what I mean. I like that whole adventure life, ya know?" he was openly flattering.

"Yeah, but the adventure has a price. I lost my damn glove out there in a thorn bush," Cleo said, showing Eric her exposed hand.

"Who cares, right? There's plenty in the house. Anyone says anything, I'll just say I needed a condom for Jay." He joked, "That'll have them flipping out," he laughed at his own joke. Cleo couldn't help but chuckle a little herself.

She kinda liked this white boy.

He quickly rolled the weed and took several long puffs making small talk about teenage things. Cleo listened to his words while making sure not to stand downwind of the smoke. Soon enough, they were back inside.

"Hey, you're pretty cool; you gonna be back? We can step out again if you do. My boy's bringing me some good Kush for my birthday ... like primo smoke."

"Sorry, I'm only here as a substitute."

"Well, 'substitute' you could teach my folks how to just chill and be cool about stuff. Anyways, see you again, maybe," he said as he left the foyer and headed to his wing of the place.

"Maybe," she said with a slight smile. She kinda liked this white boy.

Instead of walking into the hall leading to the master bedroom, Cleo grabbed some extra gloves and headed toward the parlor. She didn't want to risk heading back down the main hallway for fear a camera would have seen her cleaning the same place twice. She doubted there were any cameras in the place where Eric moved around, but she wanted to be sure. After briefly pretending to be cleaning, she spotted a cigar case: exactly what she was looking for. She slipped two cigars into her pocket and headed towards the rear bathroom.

Spending time with Eric had thwarted her plans but had given her an idea. Once she'd secured the door and checked for cameras, she reached in her pocket, pulled out the cigars, and carefully unwrapped them. Once she had them unwrapped enough, she carefully pulled out her "lost" glove and unrolled it, revealing a hand full of poison ivy leaves she'd quickly grabbed from the woods while searching for Eric's rolling paper.

She filled each Cigar and rerolled silently, thanking Bolo for one of the few skilled he'd taught her over the years. Using one of Eric's pilfered matches and sink water, she resealed each Cigar, and once satisfied, she placed them back into the top of the humidor in Mr. Lester's lounge.

She knew his morning smoke would be his last. After disposing of her gloves and grabbing her relevant paperwork, she disappeared into the night. Despite the distraction, Cleo had done her job.

\I'LL SEEYOUSOON\ was the text she sent Prescott indicating the mission was complete, but the result would be delayed.

\NOT SOON ENOUGH\ was the response.

When Sienna woke the next day, it felt like she'd dreamed the whole mission. Her morning stretch felt like heaven after getting to sleep so late. Living a double life can do that to you, but there was money to be made and bad people to put down. She grabbed her phone to check her messages when she read the headlines.

BELOVED REAL ESTATE MOGUUL FOUND DEAD

"Easy work," she mused as she read the story.

One of the city's prominent real estate owners and affluential businessmen, Jay E. Lester, and the latest heir to the Lester estate Eric Lester were found dead in their home....

"What?!" Sienna thought as she read on it turned out that Mr. Lester, detestable as he was, seemed to love his grandson. He wanted to demonstrate that love by sharing the boy's first Cigar on his 17th birthday. Sienna felt her heart sink. This wasn't the plan. This wasn't the way Cleo would want things. Hot tears began to stain her cheeks as she wondered if the young man that shared a moment with her as rebels, outcast, and equals would have been the one to change the Lester name. She knew now that she'd ended a reign of corruption and, in the same breath, stunted the hope of change. The ice-cold feeling in her chest is something she'd thought she'd gotten rid of long ago. The weight of her *other* life was almost too much to bear.

Damn ... She'll kinda miss that white boy.

ten
fishscale

AS RICO MADE his way from the CABAL to his home for what could be one of the last times, he looked out the window where he could see the environment go from privileged to destitute in a few miles of roadway. For him, passing through the suburbs with their two-story homes and medium to large front yards every day still felt new. The world of the shiny suburbs is a pool in the summer: It was designed to keep you afloat. You were meant to swim and keep your head above water. It was designed so that anyone with any minimal preparation could survive the ebbs and flows of the environment without any real danger.

Moreover, a pool is designed to allow multiple swimmers at one time. Much like suburban success, getting out and rising above the pool waters takes some effort, but can be done with enough strength and skill. Even if you fail and fall back in, you aren't at the bottom; you're merely still afloat. Very few people drown, and those who do are typically doing something unusual or are surrounded by unusual circumstances. A person swimming in the suburban currents can even see the hi-dive and those rising to the top. They clap and applaud even as they're being looked down on because they know if they put their mind to it, they could pull themselves up and make the climb. If someone gets to the top and plummets down, it's ok because that just means there's more room on the high dive.

Growing up in the lower-middle-class neighborhood of Lincoln Way wasn't easy, but it was the only life Rico knew. When your life is based on such a small environment, invisible walls around you feel like an electric fence. A person can grow but only so much. A person can develop but only so far. The competition is concentrated to keep it fierce, but ultimately nobody wins. Soon enough, the idea of what it means to win is eroded.

Almost no one owns a home (much less with a pool). The few who own homes have lived in them long enough to see the deterioration of the place they grew up in without the means to finance the maintenance. They get to watch their family legacy die, knowing they're the lucky few.

The Projects were an even worse story. As with most large subsections of the city, Lincoln-Way was home to the Martin Van Buren housing project. As children Rico and Sienna had played in the MVB more times than they could count. They were regular members of the Boys and Girls Club, where Rico loved to play basketball and swim in the public pool. The innocent eyes of a child couldn't grasp the conditions around them. Rico didn't understand what it meant to be poor until high school. It was then that he began to understand society and where he'd fit. His mother would tell him he could be whatever he wanted to be. Gladys was a stickler for reading and writing. She'd read him poetry and sing songs on the radio.

They'd watch movies together, and she'd explain the intricacies of the plot. Rico knew that those lessons made him the analytical person he was today. Eventually, as he got older, he became the one explaining things to her. It was a bittersweet memory.

"What are you thinking about?" Adonis asked, looking in the rearview mirror making brief eye contact with Rico.

"Shit's crazy, bruh. I've never lived anywhere but here. They gave me a key to one of the penthouses. I wanna go, but I feel like if I do, I'll be in somebody's pockets," Rico said while looking back out the window.

"What are you gonna do?"

"What would you do?"

Adonis thought for a minute, "I think no matter what you do, you're in somebody's pockets. That seems to be the way things work. Didn't you say you worked at a grocery store? You were in someone's pocket. When I played football, I was in someone's pocket, and once I got hurt, I was emptied out."

Rico was silent. He'd rarely heard Adonis talk about his time playing football. Even now, Adonis looked like he could still be playing. He wasn't a bodybuilder by any means, but he looked like a soldier: in generally good shape. His injury derailed his career, and Rico could only guess how promising that career could have been. He never asked Adonis about it. He had a feeling it was a sore subject.

"I wouldn't look at it like that. You make it sound like you're some kinda trash to be thrown away whenever someone feels like it. Look at you now, though. You're not rich, but you're doing pretty good. You pushing this Range, and you have a crib downtown: some clean shit. Mike told me you were in Scottsdale towers or some shit like that. I think that's dope. You're where I was *trying* to be."

Adonis gave a brief laugh, "I'm working to keep shit going. I have to do shit to make sure I'm good, but if the CABAL falls apart..." He trailed off. "You looked out. When you asked Mr. P to make me your right-hand man, it put me in a different position. Now people don't just see me as a driver. I'm doing better, but I'm still a worker. I'm not saying I'm fucked up. I'm doing right, but I'm assisting the assistant. I'm a driver, not the one driven. The flip side of that is that I'm getting more pay, and I'm looked at and handled with respect. So, I'm still in some-body's pocket. I'm just in there on my own terms."

Rico thought briefly, "That makes sense, but that only leaves one question."

"What's that?"

"Who wears the pants?"

They spent the rest of the drive-in silence playing lo-fi music. Rico didn't know exactly what he was walking into, but he knew he couldn't break his stride, not yet. The CABAL was full of glitz and glam, but Rico's first engagement with Prescott and his observation of Money Mike's daily activity told him that the underworld was as much a part of the building as the plumbing.

"Aye, Don, you ever kick it in L Dubb?"

"Nah, not really. I used to mess with a chick that stayed in MVB, but she was too ratchet. Ass was fat though."

"Well looks like I won't be here as much. I got a lot of stuff to do to get ready to move. And I am staying with my sister. I gotta see if she wants to come or not. Before I even worry about all that, I'm dying to have a fish plate from Alex. The fish be jumping, bro. Slide me over there, and let's grab some food. I know you gotta be hungry too."

"Yeah, I could eat. I like to smoke when I eat, though. Is that cool?"

"Yeah, bruh, we kick it. I'll get you right."

After a short drive, they arrived at Alex's Ribs and Fish. The unassuming building was at the same time a Bar and a Restaurant. When Rico walked in, he was greeted by a familiar face.

"Well, look who pulled up in the fly truck with a cute driver looking like some kinda boss." A voice cracked from the entrance.

"Sup, Monica," Rico said, looking down.

"Nothing much just whippin' up this fish scale ya dig. What y'all want?" Monica said jokingly.

At 5'3, Monica was a part of the neighborhood as Alex's Ribs. Sure, she got around, but Rico figured it was because she worked in a place that everyone loved. She wasn't shy and loud, but she was fun and treated everyone like an old friend. Monica knew secrets many women didn't know: how to be friends with a man. She knew how to control boundaries. She got around, but it was mostly on her own terms, and she was rarely involved in drama. Rico had known her since junior high, and they'd even fooled around a few times in High School, but for the most part, they were friends even though Sienna disapproved.

"Let me get some trout."

"We outta trout, but we have some whiting left."

"Let me get some whiting, sweet potato fries, and a sweet tea. What you want Don?" Rico asked, looking up.

"Hold up, Rude, aren't you gonna introduce us or you too good now?" Monica said, somewhat incensed. "N-T-ways, I'm Monica, this is Alex's, and everything is good that I cook. If you looking for my number on the menu, it ain't there, but if you ask nicely, you may find it Mr. Don."

"Um," Adonis said as Rico rolled his eyes and Monica revealed in Adonis's nervousness.

"Can I get the same thing but with regular fries"

"No. Cause if it has regular fries, it's not the same thing, is it?"

"Man, you know what he means," Rico said, sucking his teeth.

"I'm just messing with him, damn. I'm playing with you, boo. You gonna eat here, you gotta loosen up. Hold up," she said after sniffing the air. "You got some grass on you?"

"Yeah, I smoked outside. Is it strong?" Adonis asked with a smirk. "I got another blunt if you trying to smoke."

"Shit, I'm trying to smoke," Alex yelled from the kitchen jokingly.

Monica smiled, "I'm good. I'm on the clock right now, but it looks like you'll fit in here just fine. Now let me grab these plates."

With that, Rico and Adonis sat down and grabbed some plates. They were halfway through their meal when Rico heard another familiar voice.

"Rick ... Ricky ... Ricky ... Rico Suave"

Rico turned to see Old June Bug. "W'hat's up, June."

"Hello, Mr. President," June said, straightening up and giving a salute. "Might I bother you for a dollar, sir?"

"June Bug, you supposed to be sweeping, not bothering customers," Monica yelled from the kitchen.

"It's cool. I'm glad to see you June. I got a question. A penny for your thoughts," Rico said, pulling out a $5 bill."

"Yes, Mr. President, I will take that mighty fine sister of yours on a date in that fancy car you rode up in," June said with a second salute.

"Yeah, right," Rico laughed. "Seriously, you get around, and you see a lot. If someone offered for you to move into their house would you do it? I know you have your own spot, but what if a stranger asked you to move into a nice house they owned. Would you go?"

"Let me think. Well, you gotta be careful when things are given to you free. Ain't nothing free on God's earth. Everything cost. Look at me. I go around getting my hustle on sweeping floors and whatever to keep a few dollars in my pocket. Even when I ask to hold a lil something, I trade advice for it. Naw ain't nothing free. You just gotta know the cost. Cause you always pay the piper. And if you don't know the cost, ya better keep you a few dollars in ya back pocket in case the cost get high."

Rico pondered briefly. "Aye, Monica, can I get a Beer."

"What kind?" the disembodied voice responded.

"What kind of beer do you like, June Bug?"

"The kind with alcohol in it, Mr. President."

"Let me get a Budweiser. Put it on my ticket and give it to June."

"He done finessed you out a beer, huh," Alex said, walking by whipping tables.

"Nah, I made a purchase. This is his tip."

eleven
one call away

"YOUR LOVE IS A ONE IN A MILLION" ... Sienna grabbed the phone.

"Hello."

An automated voice answered, "You have a pre-paid call from ..."

"Lo," a voice interrupted

"Press one to accept this free call." Sienna followed the instructions.

"What up with it," Bolo said in a cool voice. Hearing Bolo's voice always made Sienna's heart flutter even though she didn't know how to feel about him anymore.

"Nothing, how are you? I haven't heard from you in a minute?" she asked, feeling like a teenager again.

"I'm straight," Bolo replied, replacing the "T" with the "K." sound. "I'm just in this Bih bidding holdin' it down. A nigga ain't got too much longer to go. I'm looking at 24 months unless I catch parole. But if not, I can do these lil 24 on my head if I have to. Small thing to a giant. How you been?" Bolo asked, sounding cocky but collected.

"I've been ok. Just working and stuff like that. I'm usually pretty busy, but I make decent money doing part-time work. I've been saving, but I'm still in L Dubb for now. It's nice to hear from you." Sienna said, trying to hide the sadness in her voice.

"Yeah, it's nice to hear your voice too. I didn't want to keep banging your line and shit cause I had too long and didn't want to be in the way ya feel me."

"Bolo, you aren't In the way. If it wasn't for you ... I just wish you were home. I'm not saying we would have worked out, but if it wasn't for you I ..."

"Nah, I feel you." He cut her off. "But if it wasn't for you, I might be somewhere fucked up. Pussy ass nigga tried to cross me out. But fuck all that. We cool shit, we always gonna be cool. I just figured I'd hit you, see what was going on. I heard Rico got a little situation at the one spot."

"The CABAL," she answered.

"Yeah, that's it. Tell him to be careful with them rich ass niggas; they don't play how we play. The whole rules are different, ya dig. That nigga is cool. He's weird, but he is one of us. He just smart and shit."

"Yeah, I know. I'm watching his back. If I see anything funny, I'll let him know. Bolo, do you need anything ... like on your books or something," Sienna replied.

"Nah, I'm good. Young boss in this muhfucka. When I first got in, I linked in with some MVB niggas I knew and some other niggas around the Dubb. We have been keeping shit moving, and I just been reading and shit, hooping, running spades rapping and shit."

"Rapping? You? Let me hear some," Sienna said, interested. "Aight, it's like this:

Lemonade, everything like who pissin' Crew itchin', we juice sippin'
We molly droppin', we too lifted Pulled up with the roof missing,
I'm too exquisite, make ya bitch lick me Niggas friendly, but they really envy
You might lose your life on the road to riches Who's right when it comes to sinnin'
One life I'm just trying to live it
Making sacrifices, I'm just tryin' to get it
But they steady hatin', trying plot against me..."

"You have one minute remaining," the automated voice interrupted.

"You want to call me right back? I can pay for the call," Sienna asked. "Naw shawty, it's cool. I'm hit you some time if it's cool when I get closer to being out. I just wanted to see how you were doing. I'm holla at you."

"Bolo ..."

"Thank you for using Jail Connection. Goodbye," the automated voice interrupted.

Sienna's heart sank in her chest. She'd forgotten how much she actually missed Bolo. She almost told him she loved him, but she knew that couldn't be true. Could it? She didn't even know anymore. Maybe she was just caught up in the moment. She hoped he wouldn't wait so long to call back. He sounded more like the man she fell for than the one she grew to resent, which did not make things easier.

As Sienna made herself some lunch, Rico walked through the door. "Hey, Rico, did you have a late-night?"

"Yeah, you know how it goes. We had that show I've been telling you about."

Sienna remembered the Luke James show that was coming. She was a fan, but she couldn't make it as usual. She sometimes wished she could tell Rico why she couldn't make it, but she wanted him to be safe, and in her line of work, ignorance and safety go hand in hand.

"You need some bread? They been paying me pretty well. More than I made at Food Shark. Actually, more than I thought I'd be making."

"I'm good, actually. I've been doing pretty ok at the Job myself."

Sienna told Rico she was a CSR rep working the graveyard shift. The alibi suited her needs because there was no set work schedule, and it explained why she couldn't be reached by phone.

"That's the crazy part. We're both doing better. New jobs and new money."

"I'm not saying we can go Benz shopping," Sienna joked, trying to keep the serious tone of the conversation off-kilter. Why was Rico suddenly talking about money? They usually stayed out of each other's business. He paid for the power and utilities; she took care of the phone, internet, and insurance. It allowed them to each contribute without being in each other's pockets. Sienna knew the CABAL would change things, but with Mr. Prescott of town, she didn't exactly have anywhere to ask questions. She could have left long ago. She didn't want to leave Rico to fend for himself, and she didn't want to lose the house their mother worked so hard for.

"Nah, no Benz lol, but seriously. I got an offer to relocate ...nto the CABAL."

Sienna's heart dropped to the floor. What was that old man's game?

She was doing a good job and making money. What did they need Rico for? He said things were ok and that they just wanted to give Rico a low-level position to put some money in his pockets and keep him protected. Why would they move him in like he's some new prospect from Princeton (or Rikers, for that matter)? Was this even about her? Maybe their work with him and with her was unrelated. Sienna was running through every conversation she's had since Prescott met Rico, and there were almost no clues to get anything from.

"Rico, what made you even wanna fuck with the CABAL? I mean, of course, the money, right? I mean, did you ever ask why they wanted you or how they found you?"

Rico let the question hang in the air. He'd hoped the money would be enough for her. He didn't anticipate her asking any further questions. Who wouldn't take a position working at the CABAL? The place was a business course and music video rolled into one. Should he tell her about the things Mr. Prescott had alluded to? No. He didn't know how deep the rabbit hole went and couldn't risk involving her in things that could complicate her life until he actually had some kind of clue himself. Once he had some direction, *then* he could tell her about it. For now, it was best to stay vanilla.

"My Boss said he ran across me through my work at Food Shark. I'm guessing it must have been a hell of a reference."

"Your boss is friends with Mr. Weston?" Sienna asked in sarcastic disbelief. "And he's connected to the CABAL?"

"Well, I guess if I was running the club, I'd still have to eat."

"The CABAL *is* more than a club," Sienna quickly snapped with more emotion than she'd intended to let slip.

Rico picked up on the slip and eyed her curiously "oh yeah? Then what else *is* it?"

"Well, from what you just told me, *it* sounds like they got apartments and everything," she responded cleverly.

Rico's mind was put at ease. Sienna didn't know anything. He knew he should focus on finding out about their father and keeping her ignorant but protected.

Sienna relaxed, knowing the statement had fooled Rico for now. Mr. P was a secretive guy, but she had never known him to be a bad guy. He wasn't her enemy, nor was he hiding things from her. She just needed to see what he wanted from Rico, and she had to find out without putting Rico in harm's way.

"So, what are you gonna do?" She asked.

"I'm .... I mean ... maybe it's *time* for me to make a move. I didn't plan all this, but maybe it's God's way of telling me there's more to this shit than being an assistant manager at Food Shark. I'm not trying to say that stuff doesn't count or that I don't love the house that mom left us, but I know she didn't expect us to live in here forever. I think I want to go and see what they're offering."

"What are *you* offering?" Sienna asked cautiously.

"Shit, hard work, professionalism, I know a few people already, hustle, and loyalty."

"Sounds like you're either in the mafia or running for office. I don't think it's a bad idea. I could have moved out with the money I'm making, but I didn't want to leave you here with the bills by yourself. I know you can handle it, but I just didn't want to leave you alone, that's all."

"Well, looks like we can both get what we want. I can still pay the bills here and live there. This can be like a weekend spot to get away from things. What do you think about that?" Rico asked.

"It's not a bad idea," Sienna replied, thinking about how much easier it would be for Cleo if she lived alone.

"Aight, bet. You know any moving companies?" Rico said with a nervous smile.

"You better run down the street and ask June Bug," she joked.

They both laughed. Their secrets were intact for a while longer.

jazzy belles

LINCOLN-WAY WAS home to Rico in much the same way that most people view home. They've attached emotions and memories to the walls that have provided them shelter and comfort for so many years. Home meant family. In Rico's case, home meant the memories of his mother.

It's not that Rico didn't think of her. He thought about her so often that he'd developed calluses over his heart to numb the pain of the loss. In the beginning, it felt like there was an empty void in the world. A tear in reality that was forever exposed and painful. Death can be a nothing. The emptiness that isn't as well known to the privileged, but is all too familiar to the residents of Lincoln Way. When Rico's mother died, the world lost its color. There remained a spectrum of hues, but the warmth no longer existed. Rico knew Sienna felt the same way, although they rarely spoke of it. Rico feared that leaving the house would somehow hasten the fading of his mother's memory from his mind. After speaking to Adonis, Sienna, and even June Bug, his mind was made up. Stop focusing on who his mother was and focus on being who she wanted him to become. It was time to take a chance.

It'd been three days since Rico told Mr. Prescott that he was ready to move in. Prescott was happy with the decision and wanted to make sure the transition was smooth. He'd hired a moving company to take care of the heavy lifting and put Rico up in a fancy hotel downtown. Rico enjoyed the nice hotel but was more excited about getting into his new digs.

"Is this goodbye, or see you later?" Adonis asked as he and Rico left the Lincoln-Way for what felt like the last time.

"More like see you around. It's not like I'll never come through. I still know people here. I still have friends and family here as well. Matter of fact, can you slide me by Pappadeaux's? I need to give the key to my sister."

"I didn't know you had a sister?"

"What? You thought I was running around living alone without a girlfriend because I didn't know how to talk to women? Nah, man Sienna is cool. She knows all about me working at the club; she even knows about you." Rico said, making brief eye contact with Adonis in the rearview mirror.

Adonis laughed, "What'd you tell her about me?"

"I told her I had a driver. Big guy. 6 foot and in shape. Good deep voice and Athletic. I told her you were the only person I halfway trust at work."

"Aww shit, I guess I'll have to ..."

"Then I told her you were gay." They both laughed heartily.

Rico had felt more and more comfortable around Adonis. He'd started to look at him as a sort of surrogate brother that he'd never had. He knew the feeling was mutual, too, because while they had a good conversation regularly, Adonis was mostly quiet around everyone else. Adonis was observant and would often privately tell Rico how he felt about people, other than Mr. Prescott. Rico respected that.

They arrived at a cafe where Rico approached a table with three women. Sienna was there with who Rico recognized as Asia and Nicole. Rico didn't know much about Sienna's friends, but he'd seen them enough times to have their names, faces, and personalities down. Nicole was a tall, dark, voluptuous type that Rico knew a lot of men went for. She was sharp as a tack, but you'd never be able to tell because she was from a small town in Georgia which meant despite her high intellect, she was too loud and country for Rico's taste. Nicole might have been hard on the ears, but Rico had known her long enough to consider her a bit of a distant big sister or cousin. He respected her opinions and admired her drive. He just tried not to get her excited lest he need a hearing aid. For some reason, she reminded him of Money Mike: Loud and good-natured.

Rico didn't know Asia as well. He was weary of Asia because he found her golden skin and brown curls attractive in a way he struggled to hide despite his sensibilities. She was around Sienna's height and had the type of face that suggested innocence that Rico thought was attractive as a young man but grew to find distrustful as an adult. The preacher's daughter's look was often deception in Rico's eyes.

"Hey, Rico, you got the key?" Sienna asked, almost impatient. "Oh yeah, here you go, oh shit, my bad, this is my partner, Don."

"Don?" Nicole asked flirtatiously. "Is that short for something, or are you just a Mob boss?"

"It's Adonis," Adonis said abruptly.

"It sure is" Nicole responded, soliciting sly laughs from the other girls.

Adonis laughed in a nervous way that Rico had never seen before. Was Adonis shaken up by these girls? Sure, they were all good-looking girls, but Rico couldn't imagine the big driver being so tongue-tied at the mere thought of speaking with them. Rico and Adonis had been around plenty of good-looking women in the CABAL. Adonis, for the most part, knew how to handle himself.

"You guys hungry?" Asia asked, breaking the tension. "We ordered some drinks, but that's about it."

Sienna gave her a look and Aisa looked back at her suggesting she was only "being polite." Rico didn't really know what to make of the situation. Rico often found it hard to understand the way that women flirt. Nicole and Asia were two examples of what he was used to. Nicole was the direct type of girl that wanted everyone in the room to know she was attracted to you. She gave the physical and verbal cues that left nothing to mystery. Rico could respect this approach, but he was never a fan of women who drew attention and put you on the spot. Making your intentions clear to the room often left a man with no options because she'd laid claim and had the looks and size to intimidate other women without giving the man much of choice.

Asia seemed to be the opposite. She was the type to leave the door open for a man to step into the situation. Rico liked women that were more subtle and accommodating. Rico, like most men his age, enjoyed the hunt. Asia's offer told him that she might be willing prey. The problem was that she might have been too willing based on the look Sienna had given her.

Rico suspected that something was going on there. Was she being friendly to them specifically, or was she just available to any guy who walked up to the table? Rico knew there was such a thing as being too friendly.

"Nah, I think we better go," Adonis said, sounding like he was looking for an excuse to escape the situation.

Rico was struggling to process Adonis' actions. Maybe Adonis was nervous around Nicole, or maybe Sienna made him nervous. A lot of guys had mentioned to him how good his sister looked. Rico still remembers how she used to get in trouble for not brushing her teeth when they were kids. He couldn't see her in any other light.

"Yeah, he's right. I'll catch up with you when I finish moving," Rico said, making eye contact with Sienna. "See you around," he said, making eye contact with Asia. Rico was no slouch at flirting either.

As Rico and Adonis began to drive away, Rico spoke up.

"Damn Don, Nicole looked like she was choosing," he said with a slight chuckle.

Adonis didn't respond. He seemed deep in thought.

"I mean, you could do worse, bruh Nicole kinda bad," Rico continued leaving room for response.

"The girl you gave the key to. That's your sister?" Adonis asked, keeping his eyes on the road.

"Yeah, but Sienna lame for real don't let the make-up fool you," he said the way brothers of attractive women are known to.

Adonis remained stoic as ever, "I swear I've seen her before."

76

thirteen
quiet storm

Years Ago ...

WATCHING Bolo get sentenced was the hardest thing Sienna had ever experienced. She'd never been inside a courtroom, and the atmosphere was cold and aggressively unfriendly. For the residents of Lincoln Way, the courtroom was looked at in much of the same way most of society looked at a funeral parlor. This was a place of corruption and injustice. This was a place where if your skin was anything but white, you'd never have a chance at receiving justice or mercy. Sienna knew Bolo didn't stand a chance when she looked into the eyes of the judge. The judge couldn't even be bothered to pronounce Bolo's name right. He wasn't interested in the case or the evidence. He came to do one thing only: put Bolo in prison.

The entire trial left Sienna physically and emotionally drained. The judge was cold and calculated when handing down the 10-year sentence. Bob wouldn't be out until they were all in their late 20's or 30's. With the gavel pounding, the judge had taken away any chance Bolo had at ever living a normal life. What was his crime really? In reality, Bolo had done nothing wrong. He went into a weed spot where people were trying to kill him, and now, he's been found guilty of manslaughter. It was hard to pin the stabbed man on him, but the gun's prints pinned him to the shooting in the trap spot. Sienna could hardly breathe. She was suffocating with the guilt she felt, and as she tried to clear her head, she found herself aimlessly walking downtown. "So, you're the girl-friend," she heard coming from a voice behind her.

She almost ran. The sound was so deep and abrupt that she didn't know how to react. She stopped and spun in a slow circle. She slowly turned around to find no one there.

"Look, I don't have any money, so leave me alone. I got my cell on speed dial to the police." As she spoke, she began to question how well her lies were landing. Bolo had enemies, and beyond that, she was a pretty girl walking downtown at night. She knew better, but she'd been so blinded by grief and regret that she'd temporarily lost her way. Now she was in an unfamiliar part of the city and hearing voices.

"No money? Like I'd believe that. I bet you don't even know the number to the police station so you can stop flexing with your phone."

Sienna was trying to pinpoint where the voice was coming from. It sounded like it was coming from an ally between the buildings, but she wasn't keen on investigating.

As she looked around, she noticed a piece of broken wood, a 2x4 with what looked like nails driven through it. Maybe someone had broken a wooden palate. She carefully approached it and grabbed the makeshift weapon.

"You better leave me the fuck alone," she said in a voice, not like her own.

"You act like a cornered cat that found its claws. What do you plan to do with that?" This time the voice was directly behind her.

As she turned to swing the make-shift weapon, the mysterious man behind her grabbed her, not unlike a soldier would grab a person being disarmed: one arm on her weapon-wielding wrist and the other around her throat.

"Now what?" the stranger mocked. "Having a fight isn't enough. You have to have an advantage, shawty. You not slick enough for that."

As the arm around her throat tightened, Sienna had to think back to what she knew about her attacker so far. She knew that he was a man by the depth in his voice. The man's strength was naturally greater than

Sienna, but he wasn't a big man. He was more lean and tall than anything. This told her the strength in the grip came from the technique, not raw power. His accent told her he was from the deep south and not a metropolitan area. Likely a small town, not completely rural. Sienna spoke her next thought through bated breath.

"If you wanted to kill me, you'd have done it by now. If you wanted to rob me, you'd be halfway done. What do you want?"

"I was trying to get your attention."

"You got it ... I'm all ears."

"That last shit you did was a C- at best. Oh, it was clever the way you used the pens. I also thought it was dope how you managed to get away scott-free with every penny in the house and no one even suspects you. You were even bold enough to come to the trial. You're just bold as fuck now, huh? Your mistake was not knowing shit about who you were dealing with."

The man loosened his grip just enough for Sienna to catch her breath but not quite enough to scream in any way that would matter. More than that, she was blindsided by the deluge of information this new stranger was providing. She had to find a way to make him talk. Time to go for broke.

"If you know all that, then you know not to fuck with me.nYou also know who my boyfriend is."

"Yeah, I know who he is," the stranger replied, "he's a dog."

Sienna almost said, "You ain't lying," but thought better of it.

"Not the kind of dog you think he is. He's like a real dog, a wolf: He's aggressive and tough from being alone and self-sufficient even though he longs for a pack. He's protective and loyal, but he lacks self-confidence, so he uses women to replenish his self-esteem. I know the type. Dangerous on his own, but if guided, he could be powerful. Everybody's some kinda animal. You two could've been my favorite animal of all. Guess what it is, and I'll tell you a secret. Don't, and you'll never make it out of this ally alive. You got about 15 seconds before you pass out."

As the Stanger's hand tightened, Sienna's mind started to panic. She started to hold her breath to calm her mind. She wasn't in a great position to fight this guy, so she had to think fast. This guy sounded like a real psycho. The type you see in movies or read about in books. She knew she was likely to be raped or worse. She had no choice but to play along. It was time to think: This isn't this guy's first rodeo. He knew what kind of guy Bolo was without indicating he knew him personally. He also seemed to know that Bolo was not a threat because he was going to jail. This guy wasn't after him; he was specifically after her, but why? Was he getting payback for the guy she stabbed? Something he said stuck out in her mind "That last shit you did was a C- at best" who the fuck grades a stabbing?

"It was you. You were on the phone."

The stranger loosened his grip slightly but said nothing.

"You were the one that sent the shooter at Bolo ..."

"Okay, I see you thinking. You earned a breath. But what is my favorite animal?"

Sienna was exhausted with all the stress and adrenaline flowing through her system. This fucking guy keeps talking about animals. How was she supposed to answer that question... unless he'd given her clues already. What had he said? A cat! He said she was in the ally like a cornered cat with claws. He also said dogs and wolves were dangerous and powerful. Suddenly the answer hit Sienna like a desperate crack of lightning.

"A Fox ..." was the last thing she murmured before she lost consciousness.

When Sienna awoke, she was in a daze. It didn't take her long to realize she was in a Walmart parking lot asleep in her own car in the middle of the night. Was it a dream? When she saw her phone, she knew it wasn't. From what she could tell, it'd been 2-3 hours from the time she left the courthouse. She closed her eyes and slowed her breathing to feel if she'd been assaulted in any way, but she hadn't. Physically she felt fine.

The trauma of what had just happened was slowly settling itself in her mind, and she could feel pin pricks of fear and rage crawling up her spine. She was assaulted forced to answer crazy questions from a psycho who had some sort of beef that was somehow related to Bolo. The last thing she can remember is desperately thinking about animals. She needed to go home. She needed to feel safe again. She needed to talk to Rico. But first, she needed her keys.

As she began to feel around her purse, she was surprised to find everything exactly how she left it except for one thing: there was an extra cell phone in her bag. When she tapped the screen, there was a picture of a Black Fox. There was no lock on the screen, but the phone had been factory reset to its default settings. No trace of anything but a text message.

/YOUR ANSWER WAS CORRECT. I KNOW YOU KNOW I COULD HAVE DONE WHATEVER I WANTED TO YOU, BUT I PROMISED TO LET YOU IN ON A SECRET IF YOU ANSWERED CORRECTLY. CALL ME. LET'S SEE IF CURIOSITY KILLS THE CAT/

Sienna wasn't sure what to do. She wanted to race home, but what if she was being watched? She couldn't have someone following her home. Especially a crazy person. Before she knew what she was doing, she'd called the number.

A familiar voice answered, "Well, looks like somebody's awake. Hope you slept good, Shawty."

"Slept fine," Sienna responded with all the false bravado she could muster.

The voice chuckled. "You shouldn't have all that attitude. You did ME wrong. You wanted to know a secret here it is: I was the voice on the phone that sent that shooter, but the hit wasn't meant for Bolo. It was for the owner of the trap spot. You know how it goes: Location, location, location? It was an easy lil setup, so I sent one of the young boys in. I saw you drop your... "dog" off and needed to let my guy know someone was in the house. The plan was to wait in the back room till Bolo left and handle his business. That was a test. You ran interference and fucked it all up. After the gun shots, I had the police called thinking Bolo had shot my guy. I needed y'all to panic so nobody would have time to communicate. Nothing like the sound of sirens to get people motivated. Bolo was collateral damage. I had to charge him to the game, but that wasn't the mission."

Sienna found his words slightly calming. "So, this was some kinda dope boy beef?"

"You not listening. Think about it. Do you think dope boys in Lincoln Way could actually afford someone like me? What I do ain't cheap. I'm trained to do what I do. I have to account for everything. This was the first time I had a situation go left. You could say you owe me money."

Everything the man said sounded like the truth. Sienna had the feeling she was being manipulated but to what end. What was the point of all this? Why was he telling her this?

"How much, how soon" Sienna responded flatly.

"Damn Shawty, straight to the point."

"No point in wasting time. You let me live twice. If I learned anything from Bolo, it was to get to the point, and the point always had to do with money. You obviously want the money more than the get back."

"You got it all wrong. I fuck with people. They're worth even more than money. Money is just used to save a life or destroy one. It's a lot of fucked up rich people that have enough money to keep being fucked up and rich. Many good poor folks don't have enough money to save themselves from violence, sickness, the government, natural disasters ... all that. You're more valuable alive, aren't you?"

"Yes, of course," Sienna said, trying to process the impromptu philosophy.

"You took my contract and killed my soldier. You should be dead already, but I fuck with how it went down. You were innocent. You read the situation, tactically found a position, tricked my guy into trusting you in an instant, and found a way to take him out without alerting people in the next room. You then left the situation with a bag full of what? Five hundred? ...and you were never even a suspect. You got some natural skill when it comes to wet work." Now curiosity had overpowered reason or self-preservation in Sienna's mind. She had spent the last few months preparing for Bolo's trial. She'd thought of herself as a victim or at least an unwilling accessory to murder until this point. The reality of Mr. Fox's viewpoint was surprisingly easy to follow. Had she ever felt bad once for the accidental murder of two men who threatened to hurt her or Bolo? She was afraid to answer that.

"I'mma be straight up. I've know you live with your brother. I've been getting info on you since that whole incident. I know y'all mama died not long ago and you just out here surviving.

You don't know shit about me! Sienna wanted to scream. She hated people bringing up her mother's death. Especially someone that didn't know her in life, but she kept silent.

"Let me put this on the table: Let me train you. That'll get rid of the life you owe me. You secure a few contracts, which will get rid of the money you owe me. In exchange, I'll put your house on a protection list. You won't ever have to worry about money. As long as you keep your end of the agreement up, you'll also be protected from the police. You won't be rich, but you'll have more money than anyone around you. This is a lifestyle. This is something I think you can do.

"You want to teach me to kill people for money?" Sienna was taken aback.

"No, I want to teach you to kill people for people. You decide what causes are worth killing over and who is worth killing for. I have my rules and principles. You'll have to come up with your own. You'll have to learn to act. You can date, but nothing serious. You can't really have any permanent life changes like marriage or children until you're out of the game or you've trained a replacement. You'll have to learn to fight. You'll have to get used to late hours and telling lies. You'll have to learn about guns, knives, poisons. You'll learn about money and power. You'll learn about the city's secrets just enough to exploit them but not enough to expose them. No one can know what you do or why. This life is yours if you want it. If you can handle it, you can trim the fat of this city and keep certain elements at bay. You can also protect yourself and your loved ones in the dark when they don't even know you're protecting them. If you're ready, say the word, and you'll train 4 nights a week starting tomorrow night. That's all I have to say; what's your answer?" Before Sienna could think, she already knew her answer. She couldn't even imagine (dream?) something like this happening to (for?) her. She opened her mouth, afraid of what she'd say next.

"What do I call you?"

"You already know. It ain't hard to guess. In the daylight, they call me Vari, but that's not the name you'll be using. I'll send a time and location to this phone tomorrow night."

"I guess I'll see you then ... Mr. Fox"

The phone went dead. Sienna knew that at that moment, everything that had happened to her the last few months was preparing her for this moment Sienna's life as she knew it was over. Her only question was: Who had she become now?

fourteen
blowin' money fast

"WHOA," Money Mike said as he answered Rico's call. He had a strange way of answering, as if he was afraid to give away his name or voice, for that matter. Smartphones and street life rarely mix well. Rico knew it stimmed from not trusting modern technology.

"Yo, what up, Mike. What good with you?"

"Shit, a nigga been up all night. I'm just getting up now. I see you living it up now. You in the big house. You walking round with ya chest poked out now, huh? I see you. Don't get too caught up in it too quickly. Niggas still gotta see what you can bring to the table."

Rico knew not to rest on his laurels, but he was slightly caught off guard by Mike's undercut at the end of the string of compliments. "What do you mean? I'm putting in work; you see what I'm doing for the lounge."

"Yeah, but the lounge was what I brought to the table. That idea was what I brought to the CABAL situation. My name on that. You work great as an assistant. I mean, you got partner potential. You may even do something ... now that niggas know you can work. The question is if you're always gonna be a worker or are you going to start busting moves on your own."

Rico hadn't thought about that. Everything he'd done up to this point had been instructed. He'd gotten into the CABAL by what can only be described as fate, and he'd maintained himself within its infrastructure by applying his management skills and street smarts. What he hadn't done was make an impact. He'd also come no closer to finding out what his father had to do with this. He was starting to feel shepherded into his current position, and he wasn't learning anything new. He felt fairly confident that Mike didn't know much about how he came to be his assistant. Mike wasn't the type to pry either.

"Don't trip, bruh; you just got here. I was really hitting you up cause I had some running around to do. I wanted to see if you were trying to get out and about."

"We got something to do for Prescott?" Rico asked.

"Nah, that's my point. You can't always do shit for the CABAL. You gotta do shit for yourself first. Once you understand how to win, you can apply those same lessons to other areas of your life. Like the CABAL. You may even find out more about your daddy's situation if you move around the city and not just the hood."

Money Mike's words rang in Rico's head as he showered and dressed. Whenever possible, Rico always showered before he left his residence. His mother preached the idea that cleanliness and class were right next to smarts on the list of things all adults needed. Now that Rico had his own personal marble and glass shower and enough clothing not to feel out of place anywhere, he was never going to allow himself to take a step backward. He got ready for the day and was down in the lobby when Mike walked out of the parking lot elevator.

"I like those shoes," Mike greeted Rico as he approached. He was looking at a white and grey pair of Air Jordan 17s. Rico always admired the way that Mike freely gave out compliments. He wasn't afraid to salute the people around him because, unlike most people, Mike was confident enough in himself not to feel belittled by the success of others. Rico guessed that kind of nature made it easy for Mike to move through so many levels of society as effortlessly as he regularly did.

"Shit, man just trying to get like you." It's always nice to return the favor. Mike's sense of style was a little flashy for Rico's taste, but Mike was always fresh in a way that got respect from his audience. Besides, who wouldn't like the Baby Blue Air Jordan 11's Mike was rocking?

As they entered the parking deck, Rico approached Mike's, Black Lexus.

The car screamed luxury with an androgynous edge.

"Nah, not that one. That's for the even numbers." Mike said, referencing his skybox placements in the lounge. "We riding in this today."

Beside the Lexus was a vehicle Rico hadn't noticed in the deck before. It was a silver Challenger. A modern muscle car with Black accents and 24-inch rims that somehow didn't look out of place or gaudy. They looked just right against the large square frame of the car.

"I'm 'bout to show you why they call me Money Mike," Mike said as he pulled out the parking lot with Rico in tow.

The day was long but far from boring. Mike was out picking up money from the product he had on the streets. He prided himself on not selling anything to the people. He supplied the suppliers. That way, he barely had to touch anything. He'd make a flight a few times a year, and he'd get enough weight to supply the city. Twice a week, he'd make his grab.

Rico wasn't sure what would happen, really. Rico was no stranger to selling drugs. He'd done it to get by for a few months at a time. A few ounces of weed and maybe a few ecstasy pills between jobs but nothing that required so much clientele outside of Lincoln Way and only when he was seriously desperate.

Each stop was different, with a different person handing him money. They started at the University. As they prepared to get out, Rico locked and loaded his newly acquired P95 Ruger.

"It ain't gonna be nothing like that, bruh. These my folks." Mike said while grabbing his Glock. "I'm saying always bring something to protect yourself, but your posture is too stiff, and you talk too proper. I be watching you at the club all the time."

"What? If you think somebody might try me, I got something real for them. They don't know me," Rico spat, feeling slighted by the remark.

"But they know me. I don't get played with out here. I get my respect cause niggas know my reputation for getting money and keeping my folks fed. Niggas can get around you and know you're not pussy. That's not the problem. The problem is that you are so no non-sense

87

they'll be scared of you. You are too smart and militant. Niggas don't know what to do with you You have to learn to make people feel comfortable around you without you being too comfortable around them."

The whole thing always played out like a social call. Mike walked in and sat down, pulled out a bottle of soda he'd bought from the store, and started debating sports with a bunch of guys that looked like Kodak Black's entourage. The gold teeth and dreadlocks were all smiles. They weren't just engaging with him; they looked up to him. It all made sense. Money Mike wasn't as rich as a big-name rapper, but he was pulling in what Rico would guess was approaching six figures. He had all the clout from his position at the lounge and respect for his work on the street. He had the cars and clothes. Even Rico knew a female or two were regularly coming to the club to see him. They stayed at the university for maybe half an hour. The socializing took around twenty-eight minutes. The collection was a two-minute process that went by so fast you could barely see it happen.

As they headed to the next location, Rico asked why deal with young guys.

Mike explained that the streets would always be the streets. The underworld is a part of human history. Supplying an even distribution at different levels allowed him to cut down on wars and theft. Mike believed dope boys ran the world. Rico knew better than that, and frankly, so did Mike (but who doesn't want to be proud of what they do?), so Rico humored his ideas. Drug dealers were a large part of the economy but not quite as large of a portion as Mike liked to believe. Rico understood that Mike had to look at the world this way to succeed in what he did.

"Aight, bruh, this next spot I'm 'bout to take you to is an AMG Boyz spot. I fuck with some of the big homies there called the Cuz. We got Big Cuz and Lil Cuz. They are both E Class California niggas. Big Cuz cool he a moves like a businessman. Lil Cuz is a gorilla. He gonna say or do something to see where you at. I know you straight, though."

Am I gonna have to shoot one of these niggas? Rico thought to himself. He'd lived in Lincoln-Way long enough to know it's a kill or be killed life sometimes. He wasn't dying to get in a shootout with AMG over some perceived slight, but he wasn't going out without a fight, and he also had Mike to look after. Mike was right about one thing: Rico wasn't comfortable with these people. He felt like Mike might be too comfortable as if he couldn't be double-crossed. Rico knew he'd have to watch people's eyes and play it by ear.

They pulled up to a restaurant just as the sun finished setting. The place was decent enough to have outdoor seating but not valet parking. Mike didn't go through the front door. He stepped over the guard rail and sat at a table with two guys.0 ne guy was bald and dark. He sounded very country and was all jokes, but Rico knew a convict when he was near one.

"Hey, Rico, this my playa partner Wiz. He's a country nigga from Alabama, but he'll hop on that bus and make it happen. I've been fucking with him for 6 or 7 years."

"Shit mo' like sebbin ask me. I'm just a creature of habit. Nothing better than getting money and skeetin' in ya old lady," Wiz said with a smile, offering Mike a cigarette.

The other man didn't say a word. Rico couldn't read his eyes either. He was quiet ... almost smoldering. Mike was the first to speak.

"Don't sweat it, Lil Cuz. niggas got what a half a bag? They can have that shit. The nigga is probably long gone; at this point, we got a couple dollars off him. Let's just keep it pushing."

Lil Cuz made eye contact with Rico. "What's up this? You brought ya mans from the club?" he said to Mike without breaking eye contact with Rico. Rico was a lot of things, but one thing he wasn't was easily intimidated. He answered before Mike could.

"Yea, I work at the club. I'm from Lincoln Way."

"Oh, you from the Dubb, huh? What's that mean? Does that mean you got some fire on you? You think cause you strapped, nobody can reach out and touch you?" Lil Cuz had created tension that wouldn't easily be broken. Rico knew he was frustrated about whatever he and Mike were talking about and wanted to vent. He was looking in the wrong direction. Rico had already sized Lil Cuz up. He knew he could take him in a fight, but he'd never leave the restaurant alive if guns came out. He also knew neither would Lil Cuz.

Rico returned Lil Cuz's gaze, "Not and live to tell it."

The Tension in the air was thick. Rico knew Lil Cuz wasn't putting on a show. He was ready to act on his words. Rico prepared himself to shoot at the first move Lil Cuz made.

Lil Cuz let his gaze linger, and then in the next instant, he burst out laughing. Rico didn't know what to make of it. He was rigid and caught off guard.

"I fuck with him," Lil Cuz said, still laughing and turning to Money Mike.

"What y'all drinking."

After leaving the restaurant, it was time for the last stop. "Aight, everything going smooth. I like this. I may need you to ride with me more often. Today is a good day. I may go home and fuck on som' tonight," Mike said in an uncharacteristically jovial way.

Rico had been in his head going over the events of the day. "What was up with ya, boy? Think it's gonna be a problem."

"Nah, you tripping; he was just fucking with you to see if you'd shake. He does it all the time. He cool, but he ain't pie, and he wants to make sure you ain't either."

Rico always found the term "pie" hilarious. Being called punk or a pussy or even a bitch was one thing, but "pie" added an element of comedy to the insult that Rico found amusing.

"Oh, shit, I'm glad you've been with me all day. I almost forgot. I'm supposed to be linking up with my man on the 3rd floor, and I wanted you there so I could introduce you to him."

"Oh yeah? Who's that?" Rico's curiosity was getting the better of him. He was used to meeting new people at the CABAL, especially the lounge itself, but the idea of heading to the 3rd floor caught his attention. The third floor of the CABAL was the studio floor. He'd heard about it but had never had the time or a reason to explore. Seems like now would be his chance.

"I know you fuck with the music shit. I used to fuck with that shit, too, back in the day. I actually went on tour with Jeezy and all that, but I focused on the streets. You know how it goes."

"You rapped?" Rico asked, genuinely curious.

"Hell yeah, nigga I was the first one out here with his own studio in the basement. We would trap out the spot and record in the bottom. Niggas couldn't fuck with me on the mic."

"I bet I could," Rico mumbled under his breath half-heartedly.

"What don't tell me you can rap? Like, can you rap, or can you rap rap?Let me hear something?"

"Aight bet:

This is not a remix; it's just the mixed addition
I let the headlights glow and hit the switch ignition
Tryin' get to a Minaj and get the chicks to clickin'
Heard you on a paper chase; well, I ain't on a different mission
I'm on the road to riches trying not to skip the distance
Get rich in an instant the oil slides against the piston
Ash the blunt inhale the tire smoke
It's just as lifting up as music pumping out our system
I ride by they wish the car that they were in was this one
But still, I give it up to anyone that stops to listen
Middle finger got me flicking off the competition
Thinking bout when I wished that I had a pot to piss in..."

Mike was silent for a moment. "The fuck you running around the Dub for if you out here sounding like Nas or some shit? You supposed to be in somebody's studio."

Rico laughed, "Nah, I just love to do it. I'm not trying to be a rapper; I just like rapping. You feel me."

"Oh, aight, I get that. I'm not a freestyler, but I can damn sure put a song together. Check me out."

The rest of how they listened to Mike's mixtape form a few years back. Mike's music was a product of his time. It was big flashy trap music with braggadocio lyrics about selling drugs, killing enemies, buying cars, and being chased by women. The subject matter was as cliche as it gets, but Rico had to admit Mike could have easily given someone like Young Jeezy or Gucci Mane a run for his money.

fifteen
check

IT DIDN'T TAKE LONG for Rico and Mike to get to the CABAL elevator. It was dark by now, which was usually when all the main engineers were finishing with the local talent and working with the more well-known celebrities. Mike had told Rico he wanted to introduce him to someone but never said who. Rico felt that if Mike wanted him to know the name, he would have told him. Rico decided to just play it by ear. What was the rush anyway?

When they arrived at the 3rd floor, the elevator doors opened, and the entire hall was grey, red, and white. Mable floor had been replaced by carpet Even the walls seemed to have a sort of covering. Rico could see soundproofing strategically placed to optimize sound though out the floor. But why would the entire hall be soundproofed? Rico's thoughts were shaken by a voice he'd recognized.

"What?! Bitch ass nigga know we still had to finish that song. I ain't got time to be playing with his ass. I swear to God I'm finna kick this bitch down and take his shit. On my mamma, I'm..."

"Don't put something on yo mama if you know you not gonna be able to pay for it," Mike said to the irate young man. "What's the problem?"

"Aye OG on GOD, this bitch ass nigga playing with me. I had a session today that was supposed to start now, and this nigga isn't even here. I got a deadline I have to keep, and I got a show tonight."

"Nigga you do NOT have a show tonight."

"Aight, Nah, I don't," the man said sheepishly after a moment of silence, "but I *do* have some hoes I'm supposed to link up with tonight. Bruh, I ain't trying to be sitting up here waiting on a session. I called this nigga and pulled up early to do this real quick and have time to put on some drip and make a scene. You know how it goes."

Rico recognized the man yelling as an up-and-coming rapper known simply as "Fresh" but spelled with an "x" in place of an "e."

Rico took the opportunity to make his presence known. "Hell yeah, I would have been mad too. Who were you waiting for? Maybe we can figure something out."

"You feel me? I'm righteously mad as fuck."

"Tell you what, we'll take care of your session, and you can have a box for tonight, but in exchange, you gotta bring an extra girl for me and premier your song at the lounge tonight," Rico said with the grace of an experienced negotiator.

"Aright Bet, my manager might trip, so we gonna have to say the shit leaked, and we just had to gon' head and let it play. As far as hoes... nigga I'm Frxsh. I can have some hoes on the way in 15 mins."

Money Mike chuckled to himself at Rico's solutions. He found it amusing that Rico inserted himself in every situation and always came out the other side with some sort of personal gain. After unlocking the studio entrance, he pulled his cell and made a phone call.

Rico stepped into the studio and found it humble but intimidating at the same time. It looked the way he'd seen in music videos. The walls were decorated in 2- or 3-foot squares that he knew were for keeping the sound waves from bouncing off the walls. There was a large leather couch and two leather computer chairs. The head engineer's chair was obvious due to the visible wear and softened leather. Near the couch was a mini fridge with a box of mini potato chips, snack cakes, and blunt wraps on top. Rico thought that the setup was designed for a person to be comfortable for hours. The room's centerpiece was a very large grey desk coupled with a compact digital keyboard making an "L" shape. The wide desk was multitiered with 3 levels of counter space designed to place large speakers and computer components. Rico could see the first level had a fancy keyboard with multicolored lights that looked like it belonged to the power rangers. The mouse likewise was unique. It sat sideways with an exposed ball mechanism and more buttons than Rico had ever seen on a mouse. The second layer held several small computer components that read "Focusrite" and "tube mp." Rico wasn't sure what these pieces of equipment were for, but he was familiar with the Xbox one. This desk tier was bisected with a large apple all-in-one computer monitor that housed the internal computer components. The third Tier of the desk left a large space in the middle for the computer monitor. Rico thought it looked more like two large, elevated platforms than the third tier. Each platform had a large matching speaker that Rico could see at eye level. The whole setup had a very command station feel to it that Rico had to admit was pretty cool.

Frxsh broke the silence. "I really could record myself, but I just don't want to have to run back and forth ya feel me?"

He was pointing to a window to a connected room opposite the entrance. The door to the room was unassuming other than the large glass window that allowed Rico a view of the interior. He could see a microphone with a conductor's tripod and a barstool inside the room. The lighting in that part of the room was lined across the top and glowed with what Rico could see as a black light.

"Shit dope, ain't it?"

"Man, don't look like shit in here for real except for some water." Mike laughed as he walked into the room and opened the mini fridge door.

"That's cause water's good for you. You should drink more ya dig," a mysterious voice spoke up.

The voice coming from the entrance caught the entire room off guard. When Rico turned his head, he was surprised to see a guy around his age and height with a slightly huskier build. The man had a styled but unkept beard and dreadlocks hanging down to his jawline.

Rico noticed that there had been a strange phenomenon in the black community over the past few years. Never before had there been such self awareness that spanned the late Millennials and early Gen Z members. The '90s and early '00s had firmly cemented the idea that members of the black community could be anything they wanted to be. There were successes of people of color that stretched from the local bus driver to the President of the United States. The idea that with hard work, the system of racial prejudice and injustice could be circumvented had become a fundamental principle in the eyes of the public. There were successes in *what* you could be but failures in the idea of *who* you could be. The invention of social media gave rise to many problems with the community; however, it also allowed those without a platform to be themselves and communicate with like-minded individuals. The world was no longer alone. People in the black community didn't have to fit prescribed notions of being black. The need to *prove* yourself largely gave way to the need to *be* yourself. It gave rise to a sort of black enlightenment and even inclusion. People of color were starting to band together and create subcultures such as the Blerd (Black Nerd) culture of video gamers and anime enthusiasts, both male and female, with the fandom of the traditional nerd but with elegance, humor, and flavor that no other community could claim. The notion that it was ok to be black as well as the notion that is was ok to be homosexual was starting to take hold. The injustices faced at large by black and brown communities were being confronted head-on. Like all movements, the erosion of the old separatist, xenophobic, and bigoted society was a slow process, but the movement could be seen now better than ever in Rico's eyes. Rico thought that Money Mike was a great part of the old regime, but he wasn't as accepting or enlightened about certain aspects of the culture because he was unwilling to be. The man that walked into the room was very much the opposite. He wore a black letterman jacket over a button-down green and pink Hawaiian shirt. His prefaded black jeans covered a pair of Bright green Jordans with black laces. Rico was taken aback by the hipster in front of him but impressed by the confidence the man clearly had within himself. The man looked at him.

"Yo, what's up? I'm Jelz; nice to meet you," the man said, extending a

fist.

Rico bumped it, "What's good, man, Rico."

"Like the Puerto or like the laws they used to do mass indictments?"

The room fell silent. What kind of question was that? Rico couldn't read the man's expression.

"Nah. Like the printer company."

The man known as Jelz erupted into laughter. "I fuck with him," he said to Money Mike, who was drinking a bottle of water from the minifridge.

"Good," Mike responded, turning to Rico, "This is who I brought you to meet. Jelz runs the 3rd floor of the CABAL. He mostly handles the studios, but he's good for a few odds and ends. He used to run with the AMG but somehow ended up here."

Jelz chimed in, "Don't say somehow like it was a mystery. I started making music that was bigger than jumping niggas with the gang. I still got love for them, but my motives are different. I'm more interested in being creative. Hold up...who is that in my booth...! KNOW that ain't Frxsh. Nigga you not allowed near any of my equipment when I'm not here."

Frxsh sucked his teeth, "maaan, don't act like that. I mean, we got the stuff back, didn't we?" He then turned to Rico, "Ok, hold up before he gets to slandering my name; here's what happened: I had a couple of homeboys over here, and whatnot, and one of the people *I didn't know* grabbed a iPhone and tried to steal it. Jelz told me, and I got it back before buddy left the building. It's not like old dude got away with it. I don't see the problem."

Jelz interjected, "Yeah, you not even gonna mention the fact that you and your flunkies stomped him out and broke the damn thing. Then you and Bolo held him down and fed the broken pieces to him."

"Bruh, you know I couldn't let him steal from my partner, and you know if that nigga 'lo is involved, he gon' blitz every time. I gave you $200 to replace it, plus I tried to toss one of these hoes at you."

Jelz sat down in defeat, "Yeah, and that's why you're even allowed back in here. And hell Nahl didn't waste my time with none of them well-infected thots. Looking at Mike, "Is this nigga crazy? Fuck I look like?"

Laughing, Mike chimed in, "Yeah, Frxsh, next time you gotta have some vegan bitches with you. He would have jumped down on one of them then."

Everyone laughed, including Jelz.

"Jelz, is that your real name?" Rico said with his usual directness. "Nah, but that's what they call me. Cause I been in and out a few of 'em. Nothing bad really just loitering, destruction of public property, public intoxication ... anything I can do to get arrested."

"Arrested?" Rico asked, genuinely curious.

"Yeah, just cause a nigga get knocked don't mean he ain't still active or still useful. If a nigga needs some info or a pack and he up the street, somebody gotta get the message to 'em. Trust me, I don't do shit for free, but if the pay is good, there's nothing I can't do or get done ya dig."

Jelz pulled out a glass bowl for smoking weed and filled it as he checked the lights on the studio equipment. Mike and Frxsh were discussing women ... mostly their physical attributes. Rico was starting to like Jelz. He was a great combination of street-savvy, rebel hippy, and music professional In many ways, he was the opposite of Rico, but that also made them alike: they both represented a counterpoint to the general rabble and dead-end mentality of most residents of Lincoln Way.

whats my name

"IF YOU GON' throw punches like that you're wasting my time. I don't need someone that can't fight and can only shoot. You have to be quick on your feet and fast with your hands. Do it again"

Sienna was exhausted. It had been weeks of hearing the same stuff. It seemed to Sienna Mr. Fox had become more like Mr. Badger. Nothing she did seemed good enough or fast enough. The training had been strenuous and spontaneous all at the same time. One day it was how to get across an abandoned house without touching the floor. One day it was how to steal from a news stand. He even had the audacity to have someone come and teach her about how to apply make up properly. Not just apply it but use it to change her natural appearance. No two days were alike, but each lesson led to the next. Changing your appearance made it easier to steal from the news stand the second time. Building upper arm strength allowed her to lift herself up to the attic and get across an abandoned house. Anything that was done correctly then had to be done faster and under harsher conditions. Failure was met with a cold dead tone of a man that had very little to offer in the ways of comfort. Pity, Sienna couldn't help but find his stoic demeanor attractive at first, but his merciless stare told her he wasn't here looking for a date. He'd been teaching her the basics of how to incapacitate and escape all day.

"It's not about fighting it's about running," he'd tell her. "You ain't out there to be brave. You're out there to make shit happen and leave. That's it. You have to be able to wound or cripple anyone that sees you and can get close enough to grab you."

Fed up Sienna responded, "Damn I'm tired. I thought I was going to be helping clean up murderers and rapists. You have me training like I'm supposed to break into the damn white house."

"You may have to if you want the rapists and murders. Let's do something else real quick. Up to this point I've just been showing you want to do if things go left cause I won't have time to clean up any mess you make. Now let's see what you can do with this." Mr. Fox handed her a large black semiautomatic pistol.

Sienna had seen guns before. Who hadn't in Lincoln Way? Now, thanks to Bolo, she'd fired one as well. The only problem was that Sienna couldn't bring herself to be involved with one. Back in the day she thought they were cool. They were the accessories of bad boys. Something that thugs carried to let other guys know not to fuck with them. Now, after the incident that sent Bolo to jail, she had a very different opinion.

"Don't hold it like that. Are you scared of it?"

Sienna didn't answer. She was lost in thought about what had brought her to this point. She was outside the city in the dead of night doing some crazy ninja training and being paid for it by a mystery loner. She wasn't scared of the gun. She was scared of what she was becoming. Sienna felt like she didn't know herself anymore. She felt like her life had sped up so much it'd passed her, and now she was struggling to catch up. Training was exhausting her body and mind to the point that she spent all her time at home sleeping and nursing her sore muscles and wounds. At first, she threw herself into it to escape from her reality. It was scary but more than that it was exciting. She had a huge secret that no one knew. She was secretly becoming a bad bitch ... or at least that's how she felt sometimes. Other times she felt like she was pretending to be something that she's not. She's not some fighter, some vigilante for justice, she was lucky enough to survive a scary situation and unlucky enough for it to send her boyfriend to jail. Now she's here trying to be ... something, someone.

"What? It ain't gon' bite you shawty. I'mma show you how to hold it—"

"No. I'm ... just no. I can't do it. I can't shoot this. I can't shoot people. I'm not the Army type. I just wanted to ... I just I can't. I don't know what I'm doing. I don't want to do this anymore." Sienna pleaded to what she knew were deaf ears.

"Give it back to me," Mr. Fox said without emotion. He took the gun and sat down. The warehouse where they trained was quiet. A large room filled with gym equipment, weapons, manikins. From the outside it looked like a condemned structure, but the inside told a totally different story. Mr. Fox sat down pulling his dreads out of the hasty bun and letting hang nearly shoulder length. He pulled out a cigarette and a small torch lighter and lit it. Sienna was bracing herself for his response, but none came. He just sat there smoking his cigarette and thinking.

After 5 ruins past he broke the silence, "Ok you say you can't do this. You might be right. You can't. But let me ask you this: who can?"

Sienna thought out loud "What do you mean who can?"

"Listen shawty the only way for you to do something you wouldn't or couldn't do is to be someone else. Who says we have to be one person all the time. We have the gift of imagination. We have the knowledge of the past Just because we live normal lives doesn't mean we are limited to them. People lead double lives all the time. It's a sign of greatness if you think about it. Kings and queens aren't those people when they're with friends. Soldiers aren't soldiers when they're home with family. Trust me I should know. Think about this: do you really think my name is Mr. Fox? The truth is that it isn't just like I told you before ... but when it serves me, it is. A fox is a cunning predator that can survive in most climates and are found all over the world. They are successful hunters that have been hunted but continue to thrive. They are admired for their skills so much that the animal has become synonymous with cunning. It not about who I am it's who I need to be. I can purport to be anyone! Want hero or villain. Sienna can change her world, but she needs a partner. Who's it gon' be?"

Sienna's closed her eyes as her mind raced back through the most powerful women in history. Many names came and went but one name stuck out for its association with Power, Cunning, Savvy, and Beauty.

"Cleopatra."

seventeen
aint easy

THE CABAL WAS in full effect the night after the studio session with Frxsh and Jelz. Rico was making his rounds greeting guest and taking time to en joy the atmosphere. Why not? The entire operation had been running smoothly since he took over as assistant manager. Not that the CABAL needed the help, but Rico got the impression that rotating new blood into the environment was good for business. Why else would they allocate so many funds to brining guest artist to rock the stage? Tonight, may not be one to base the fiscal year on, however it was an opportune time to see Frxsh on stage.

Rico wasn't really that familiar with the whole Trap/Drill music scene. He grew up in the time of Jay-Z and Drake. The emergence of the Chicago drill scene had changed hustler hip-hop back into gangster rap but without the risk and reward mentality steeped in the realities of urban culture. Rap had been clothed in the idea of gaining money, power, and respect. These days those ideas had started to fray. The emphasis was now on violence in a way that Rico both admired and feared. Rico could remember being a child learning about the deaths of rappers like Tupac and the Notorious BIG. Older guys would talk endlessly about how tragic those times were. These days the death of a rapper hardly made headlines. Fame, money, and glory were the expectations of today's artist. The price for this ideal was often imprisonment or death. 50 Cent being shot was an epic story for Rico but now rappers got shot all the time. Rappers were not only the victims, but also the shooters. Careers came and went in the blink of an eye and the fans encouraged the spectacle, in Rico's mind, to the peril of the inner city. The urban culture had changed into a world of materialism, violence, and the savage struggle for power in the most impoverished areas of the inner city and across the underdeveloped rural areas.

"Yo what up wit cha now brody," Rico's thoughts were interrupted by a voice over his shoulder. He turned to see Frxsh with an outstretched hand.

"Shit man working.You know how it is. You ready to hit the stage?"

"Man, I was born ready. You gon' see" Frxsh responded confidently.

Frxsh was doing his part to live up to his name. He was dressed in a bold yet conservative way: A short sleeve tee with a foreign designer's name etched across the chest like a signature sat atop a pair of skinny jeans that had been splashed with what looked like multicolored paint. The whole outfit rested on some chunky looking Balenciaga shoes that looked like sneakers and cost as much as a month's rent in Lincoln Way. The regalia of rappers always looked great in certain environments like the mall or at a nightclub. Frxsh seemed to know that. His clothing was much more humble during his recording sessions.

"Yo I ain't forget the deal we made either." Frxsh said nodding his head toward a table sitting center stage.

Rico looked to see three women that were turned toward the opening act that looked like looked like filet mignon, but probably had the personalities of spam.

"I know you thought I'd have some black feet ratchets, but nah this ain't that. I ain't one of them. I take this music shit serious, and I don't have just anybody around me. You gotta bring something to the table and be ready to support. Plus, I don't like all that drama and shit. The one in the middle that's mine. You can take your pick from the others. Just let me know and I'll introduce her to you."

Rico recognized one of the woman as she turned to speak to the other two girls. With a smirk he points to a familiar face with straight black hair braided in a way that cost a few hundred dollars.

Frxsh smiled in agreeance, "I already knew you was gonna pick that one. You like them big word looking bitches around you, don't you? Aight bet after my set I'mma pull up with her. Don't be acting scared to jump down on her when I do. I can't give you the pussy I can only give you a leg up you feel me, but know she gon' go.You a big word kinda nigga. I fuck with that.

After the brief exchange and some words of good luck Rico headed up to the skyboxes to see how things were going with Mike.

"You just in time Cuz," Mike said with his usual nightlife demeanor. "You fuck with basketball, right? I need you to help settle some shit."

Mike led him to a booth with 4 women and 3 men, one of which Rico recognized from the last time he and Mike went out.

"What up with you bruh?" Wiz extended a hand after recognizing Rico.

Mike speaks up "Aight aight now tell this nigga Lebron is the most hated player because he the best. Niggas so stuck on Jordan they can't give my nigga his credit."

"I'm not saying that nigga ain't good hell he great he just ain't the best He top 10 ..."

"Top ten! Do you hear this fool? See you lucky y'all spending money and y'all my patnas cause that would have got you put out." The booth erupted in laughter.

Rico thought for a moment, "I'll say this. On the court Lebron is the greatest of his Generation just like Jordan was the greatest of his.He can play any position including big man. I'm not sure Jordan could run the 5 for a full quarter if need be. The question is should Lebron be considered number one or number two. That's tough but I'd say that his moves off the court make him number one in my book, because he's more than an athlete. He's one of the few celebrities that actually make a good role model; not by being conservative and standoffish like Mike but by being active."

The room fell silent for a moment. Rico didn't intend to be so maudlin. This was the time for ribbing exchanges not encyclopedic analysis. He had a habit of doing that and he wondered if his approach made him an asset or a liability for Mike in these conversations.

Mike ever the wordsmith took what he could. "See that's even more reason why he's the best! Thank you cuz this nigga just country."

Wiz responded, "Yeah, I bet I take your money after this round of the playoffs. They just gon' be calling you Mike in a minute."

Everybody laughed including Money Mike.

"Let me check the rest of the booths real quick so I can be downstairs in time to see Frxsh. I'mma holla at y'all."

After checking with the other patrons in the CABAL Rico took a seat at the bar.

"I didn't think you fucked with Frxsh like that" Adonis said pulling up a stool and handing Rico a drink.

"Actually, I kinda like dude. He's got that energy ya know? There's a lot of childish bravado but he's cool. I got a chance to chop it up with him up at the Studio. I think he's more than what he pretends to be. I think he might actually have some sense if he can grow up a little."

As if his words were a cue the music began and Frxsh hit the stage. The music was perfect for the crowd. It had energy and good vibes even though the lyrics were all about money and women and street life.

"Get sent where the clouds at,
Should have watched what he said, he can't take it back,
We on top of his head like a ball cap
Fuck around get hit with this small mac."

These things are the same things everyone rapped about Rico thought Sometimes the music should be shallow. There's a place for that kind of entertainment. Everybody isn't Lupe Fiasco the same way everybody isn't Chief Keef. Music like life is about finding a balance between those two things. Atleast that what Rico thought just before he turned his brain off and enjoyed the show.

After, leaving the stage and quickly changing Frxsh sent a message for Rico to come sit with him and his entourage in the VIP section.

"Aye y'all this my new partna Rico. I ain't know what to think about him at first but I fuck with him. He the reason y'all got to hear "Ain't Easy." I was supposed to save that one but fuck it I gave yall a sneak preview. Y'all got him to thank."

A grand introduction from the man of the hour. Rico knew better than to waste the opportunity.

"That was a dope set. Nothing we appreciate at the CABAL more than exclusivity. We have some unreleased materials of our own.

With a head nod Adonis showed up followed by 3 hosts carrying white and brown bottles.

"Whoa nah what's this" Frxsh responded.

"This is a new Clairin-Velier Vieux Sajous Cask Strength 4 Year Old Haitian Rum we've recently imported. We weren't going to reveal it until next weekend, but I figured you guys might be thirsty." Rico knew the cost would have to be offset by tonight's attendance but when word spread that Frxsh premiered his new song this weekend every competitor is going to try to usurp his throne. It was a financial gamble, but it was the cost of doing business.

"I'll have one," Rico was unsurprised by Alanna's voice. He'd recognized her as the "big word looking bih" earlier.

"Nah your drink is at the bar. I can take you if you want."

"Well, who wouldn't want that." She responded playfully.

"Ok, ok that what I'm talking about jump down then. Told y'all I fuck with him."

Rico escorted Alanna to the bar where drinks had been prepared for them. "Are you stalking me or what"

Alanna rolled her eyes, "Boy please I was stalking Frxsh"

"Well I'm sure you could do worse," he said reflectively.

"I have but with better," she responded staring directly into his eyes.

Alanna was in rare form. She was always a seductress but for the second time Rico felt like she was almost overpowering. He couldn't help but think of snatching her dress off and losing a few hours with her in his suite.

"Um this is a nice place, but the drinks are weak as fuck," She said with clear disappointment.

Rico laughed, "What happened to the new bougie sexy Alanna? You know Frxsh says you seem like a "big word" type."

"Frxsh is a little boy impressing little girls. I wouldn't touch him to throw him. Cute though. I heard about his show, so I decided to tag along with a girl that knew him. Sorry about dissing your drinks, but it's hard to be sexy with a Shirly temple."

Rico said nothing.

"Look it's not like before. *I'm* not like before. I can handle a drink. I've only had two tonight. I know I went away for a reason, but you have to know I wouldn't be here if I was still dealing with stuff. Things are different now. Better now."

"From alcohol to entourage? I don't know whether to be happy you're here or ask why you came back."

"I came back because I was better. I am better. Look at me. Really look at me." Alanna was serious.

Rico had to admit Alanna was stunning, but it was more than that. She looked like a model. The skinny vixen he knew had thickened up but kept her waist thin and arms tone. She looked like she'd been working out.

"You make a good point. Tell Cardi B's trainer I haven't seen my abs in two years. I could use the help." Rico said with a chuckle.

"Oh, I don't know…I like the way you've grown. You're bigger in a way. Not taller or more muscular. It's hard to describe. I guess you look like a man now. I don't know whether to hug you or pull your clothes off and loose a few hours at my place. Abs not required for entry."

Rico felt his mind drifting back to hotel rooms and late night visits. Locker room make out sessions and movie nights. Those thoughts threatened to block out memories of broken windows and empty glasses. Prescription pills and hidden wine bottles.

Alanna could see his hesitance, "I'm just joking damn. You're always so serious. You'd be boring if you weren't so boring."

"Maybe I need to find something that interest me." Rico responded cautiously placing his hand on her thigh. The warmth made his heart skip a beat. It wasn't like he hadn't been with women but something about Alanna was different. She was a predator. She knew how to use her eyes, words, and body in ways so subtle that she'd be driving your car in a week if you gave in. Rico wanted to turn the tables a little. Make her feel hunted.

Alanna felt the goosebumps rise as she felt the familiar touch. She was being disarmed.

"There's not enough booze in this drink for me to fall for your little charms," she teased.

Rico smiled, "I have some better ones in my room."

eighteen
hot girl summer

LINCOLN WAY WAS a town of exploitation. Everyone was either using someone or being used by someone. The people in power understood this as a principal of survival. The segregation throughout the neighborhoods were a testament to that principal. The poor were given low quality goods and heavily taxed on purchases to ensure they remained poor, and the collectors of those taxes remained rich. Neighborhoods were full of used car dealerships, predatory lenders, and liquor stores. School funding was allocated to ensure the suburban districts were given the best technology and highest pay rates while the underdeveloped sectors were given metal detectors and truant officers. Politician's pockets were lined with campaign funds provided they push the social agenda that served the purpose of their sponsors. The church preyed on people's faith and fear of death to provide guidance and spiritual healing at a premium. Was there a God? Sure, there was. There was a God the same way there are trees in the forest, however you still have to pay to get into the park. The trees don't stop the park property owners any more than God stopped those that would use his message to thicken up collection plates. If there was divine intervention it was given a full workload giving people the strength to endure the environment and still manage to find love, family, and friends. Everyone was being exploited, but some people were special cases.

"Ok Stephanie when you get a chance make sure you input the patient's information as they tell you. There's nothing like trying to remember every procedure after the fact."

Sienna fought the urge to roll her eyes. "Thank you so much this is all so new to me I think I'll have to take notes" she said with a high-pitched laugh. The clinic was small but lavish no doubt to make visitors feel comfortable.

Sienna or "Stephanie" was the new hire there to temporarily take over receptionist duties for Dr Fowler. Sienna wasn't used to roles that were so public, but she took lessons learned from listening to her friends speak about call center jobs and administrative positions to understand the basics of work flow and common business courtesies.

Dr. Christopher Fowler was a man of accomplishment. If his early work on ovarian studies hadn't propelled him on the local medical map his appearance on streaming ads made him a bit of a local celebrity. Opening the Fowler OB clinic was likely his crowning achievement. Medical school couldn't have been easy at Emory, but he still managed to impress at every level. What's more he managed to walk away from medical school debt free due to his hard work and personal investments. That leg up over his peers earned him a residency in Chicago for a few years before he settled in one of the nicer suburbs of Lincoln Way.

Dr. Fowler also had a reputation for his looks and charm. He always paid meticulous attention to his appearance. For a man in his late 30's he strived to keep a Hollywood physique. This often left the ladies swooning over his Jake Gyllenhaal features and George Clooney demeanor. Every day he'd arrive to work early so that everyone on his staff including his fellow physicians could see his neon blue Maserati Gran Turismo. Why not? He'd worked hard and earned the right to have nice things. He was not a man to take the stairs, he was a man to invent the elevator. Medical work was a labor of love, but running a clinic was business. Dr. Fowler prided himself on his ability to defy the odds and make things happen. Shining above and beyond his peers made him feel like a Jesus figure in the local medical community. Sienna knew there was more to the story than a chiseled jaw line and Tom Ford suits. It was a shock to the system when Sienna received the message that

Dr. Fowler would be her next target. There was something ugly beneath the good doctor's veneer.

In the 3 years since his practice started gaining notoriety, the number of missing persons cases had doubled statewide. There didn't seem to be a real rhyme or reason for it. Parents were receiving letters from collage age daughters saying they'd eloped or joined the military. Boyfriends would lose their girlfriends seemingly overnight with little more than a goodbye text. There were never any bodies found or suspicion of foul play, but the community hadn't felt safe in a longtime especially for young women. Sienna was here to rectify that.

"Well, if you need any assistance, I'll be right down the hall finishing the out processing and billing paperwork. Just give me a ring if you need anything. Oh, and by the way there's a Keurig in the break room...take full advantage honey."

Sienna liked her trainer, Jennifer. She was...bubbly. Sienna wondered if that kind of ostensibly jovial attitude was a sign of naive weakness or a reflection of inner strength.

"Good morning, Jessica how's my sched... I'm sorry I didn't realize..."

Sienna looked up from her computer screen to see Dr. Fowler staring at her with the most perplexed look. She decided to break the ice.

She conjured up her most office friendly voice. "Good morning, doctor. Jessica's out today I'll be temping for her. I've taken the liberty of printing out your schedule for today and keeping 20 minutes between appointments to allow for some reprieve between patients."

"Well look at that," Dr. Fowler leaned in "here 5 minutes and already making me want you."

Sienna feigned ignorance "excuse me?"

"Well, who wouldn't want to hire someone that hit the ground running? Pro activity is better than no activity I always say. When my 10 o'clock gets here can you let me know? Thanks." And with that the doctor disappeared down the hall.

Sienna could hardly hold back her repulsion. She knew exactly what kind of man Christopher Fowler was. He was a narcissist and most likely a killer. That knowledge alone would cause anyone to want to leave his presence, but somehow the fact that he was handsome and charming made it worse. She knew she'd have to bide her time and get him alone. The task sounded easy enough.

It would be an hour before the clinic opened its doors yet there was a visitor.

"Excuse me is Dr. Fowler in?" a man asked approaching the desk.

"Yes Sir, are you here to setup an appointment for someone or..."

"I'm here to see Christopher. He's an old friend. Don't worry about it. So pretty." The man said in a thick eastern European accent as he walked past the desk toward Dr. Fowler's office.

Sienna wasn't sure what to do. The man was large enough, but he was not a large man. Sienna sized him up to be around 6ft 190 lbs. or so. There aren't many eastern Europeans in Lincoln Way, but it's a big city. There were bound to be swaths of foreigners she wasn't aware of. That wasn't enough to bother her but the way the man complimented her was...strange. Sienna couldn't put a finger on it, but the man looked at her as if the only thing keeping him from touching her was her desk.

"Fuck around if you want, Borat," Sienna said a loud to no one but herself. She knew 10 ways to incapacitate him with the office supplies she'd strewn around her desk.

Sienna was creeped out but felt a sigh of relief upon seeing the man leave almost as suddenly as he'd arrived. As she watched him go, she noticed his face was red. He gave her a curt nod and perfunctory smile before leaving the building. Sienna couldn't help but wonder why a man like that would be here in a women's only clinic. More than that, why was his face beet red as if he'd been in an argument. She decided to drop the issue and remain focused on the task at hand. She was here for Dr. Fowler and no one else.

After, half a day of what Sienna assumed were normal operations Dr. Fowler emerged from his office wearing a white coat looking very much the part of the physician.

"Hey Stephanie can you lock the front door and help me with some files in my office. I like to lock the door so everyone can enjoy their lunch. All work and no play. You know how it goes."

"No problem, Dr. Fowler." Sienna wondered if this was the time. By her count there were 3 physicians, 3 nurses and 2 receptionists including herself and Jessica. Too many for her to risk dealing with Dr. Fowler in the daytime. She'd have to play along a while longer.

As she walked into his office, she was instantly distracted by a giant taxidermy brown bear.

Dr. Fowler spoke up, "I'm a bit of an adventurer. I scored this guy on the Appalachian trail a few years back. It reminds me that if you put your mind to it and aren't afraid to get your hands dirty, you can accomplish anything. I know that just like I know medicine."

"That's impressive Dr. Fowler. I couldn't even imagine being in the woods with an animal like that. Even looking at it now makes me nervous." Sienna tried giving her best "Santa Baby" voice.

"Well, I'm a hunter. I'm never afraid. What about you Stephanie, are you a hunter or do you prefer to be pursued?"

Sienna had to think. She didn't expect to be answering a bunch of questions from the soon to be dead Dr. Fowler. Excessive conversation humanizes people. It makes them hard to kill.

"Oh, stop with all that nonsense" a familiar voice spoke from the doorway. Jennifer stepped into the room brandishing a four-cup cardboard earner.

"Lunch has arrived. We typically have lunch on the company dime whenever we have a new face around here. The farmers market brought some fresh lemonade, and we have a couple of sandwiches from the deli." She looked at Sienna, "Here honey best lemonade in the world if you ask me.

"What kind of sandwich do you like ham or turkey?"

Sienna wasn't a Muslim, but she typically shied away from pork if she could help it.

"Wow this lemonade is good," she said taking a few sociable sips. "I'm a turkey girl. Dr. Fowler can I bring you back a sandwich from the break room?"

"Sure I'd like a turkey sandwich," he said flashing a winning smile that managed to look like a wink. He made his voice deeper as he spoke as if he was doing an Elvis impersonation.

Sienna felt creeped out but needed anything to get away from him so that she could regroup. She found his charm creepier by the second.

As she turned towards the office door, she noticed Jennifer was giving her a cold stare.

"Is something wrong-"

Sienna started to speak but everything was a blur.

"Are you ok Stephanie? You don't look well. Let's hope the lemonade wasn't too strong," Jennifer spoke in an unnaturally deep cold unfeeling voice. "What do you think Dr. Fowler?"

"I'm ok ... just ... vertigo ... or something" Sienna said as she slumped into the office chair suddenly feeling very heavy.

Dr. Fowler grabbed his note pad and,"Well as a professional courtesy I'm not going to call that a misdiagnoses but based on your physical reactions it looks like you may have ingested an extract of scopolamine. How do you feel?"

Sienna couldn't keep up with his questioning. The room started to feel warm, and she realized she was in a sort of dream state. She'd been poisoned. "Can you stop playing doctor and help me get her downstairs?" Jennifer sounded completely different now. Even through the haze Sienna knew the hard truth. She'd been set up. But by who?

"Why are you here?" Sienna felt like she'd dozed off to sleep for a second before the abrupt question woke her up. She knew a little about poison and knew she'd have to concentrate on a single point to stay focused. She bit the inside of her cheek. The shock of pain and taste of blood caused the room to clear but she could feel herself slowly slipping back into a state of defenselessness. She had to answer quickly.

"I'm a temp. Here to work. Your girl not here."

A now menacing Jennifer spoke, "Cute but we requested a temp from our ... internal supply channels. I'm not sure why you're here but I do know we didn't request you. You don't have any documentation on you. I checked your wallet, and it was completely empty. Your purse is filled with nothing special."

"The girl said she came to work. No need to be harsh. Nothing like an honest day's work. I've built my practice on it. I won't get much for you but you're in good shape. Pretty enough. You look like expensive stuff, but you have the eyes of one of those Lincoln Way girls. I'm sure you've had to do unscrupulous things in your time to survive. Think of it like this. Now you'll be doing things to ensure *our* survival. You see whatever-your-name-is I know you're not with the feds. I have friends in high places. Maybe you're with a rival. Maybe you're curious. Who knows? All I know is that you're not here by accident. You seem to be interested in what it's like behind the scenes of my humble practice. Fair enough. I'm going to make sure you get you money's worth."

Dr. Fowler approached Sienna putting his face inches from Her's speaking in a threating gravely whisper. "Personally, I wouldn't mind keeping you for myself. You thought you could come in here and tear down what I've built. You're dead wrong. By the time my beneficiaries are done with you and this body the mental trauma alone will leave you so incapacitated we could drop you off in whatever ghetto you're from and you won't be able to think clearly enough to tell anyone. You'll be used up. Talking to yourself suffering near fatal withdrawal. I told you I was a hunter. I also know when I'm being hunted."

Sienna's heart was starting to race. She was in deep. Even her employer wouldn't suspect anything for at least 2 hours. She couldn't reach her phone. If she hadn't been drugged taking these two would be child's play. For now she needed a plan and she only had seconds to think of one.

Her thoughts were interrupted by a knock at the door. Nurse Jennifer stepped out to meet the stranger. Just as suddenly as she'd stepped out, she stepped back in. Sienna couldn't see what was happening but the look on Dr. Fowler's face was in full panic.

"Who the fuck are you?! Do you know who you're dealing with?"

In a black flash a figure had crossed the room and struck him. He slumped on the floor as blood trickled down his chest from his neck staining the carpet.

"Fox," Sienna thought. "Thank God he's been secretly watching my progress on this hit." Sienna looked to meet the gaze of her savior wondering if he was truly the friend and trainer she imagined or a new foe.

A woman's voice spoke "Sloppy, slow, easy to trick. No escape plan, no equipment, not even an EpiPen or adrenaline shot. This is my world little girl. This isn't the place for Nancey Drew. I've been watching this place for days. You're lucky I was ready to make my move, or you would be headed to a slave trade in South America maybe Asia. What would Rico have done I wonder?"

Sienna tried to focus but the woman's hair was bound like a doctor in for surgery. Hat, gloves, mask...the full kit. The drugs caused the woman's voice to sound deep and slow. Her eyes were gray contact lenses. Just as quickly as she had entered the room she was gone.

Speaking would be pointless, but Sienna knew she had to get out of there quickly. She stumbled to the front of the building to find her phone. She quickly text Fox.

/SHOWS OVER. MOVIE WASN'T GREAT. TOO MANY CRITICS/

/POST CREDIT SCENE TAKES 15/

Sienna slowly headed to the meeting point with more questions than answers.

nineteen
doing damage

FRIENDSHIP WAS hard to come by in Lincoln Way. The kill or be killed atmosphere was a direct reflection of the survival culture. Often, those would-be friends ended up stepping on each other's toes or flat out betraying each other for the pursuit of similar interest. Friendship meant vulnerability. It meant that a person's well-being wasn't the only bargaining chip that could be used to manipulate them. Rico had seen friends come and go over the years. Sometimes these brief reprieves in loneliness only lasted long enough to satiate a need for human interaction that couldn't be gleaned from the affection a woman could provide. Sure, Rico had girlfriends over the years, but like Alanna, they often ended up following a path that separated them for long periods of time. It was then that Rico was forced to look around him and remember who his friends were.

Black was his closest friend. He grew up with Rico. Beyond school, they were always seen together. Rico's mother didn't exactly approve of Black, but she always understood that Rico had love for him. She also knew that Black loved Rico too in his own way. In Lincoln Way, the highest form of love was protection. Black felt like Rico was too forgiving and calculating to survive in a neighborhood full of desperation and aggression. He'd often pick fights with Rico just to make sure Rico knew how to protect himself. Rico was a fighter; Black knew that

116

much but Rico always fought with emotion. He'd overlook strangers but if Black was involved Rico's emotions would dictate his actions. Black would often tell Rico that waiting until someone pushed you isn't enough. A man must meet aggression halfway. Before Black died, he'd given Rico a Bersa .380 semi-automatic pistol. "I call this bitch silver cause she ready to go soon as I am. It ain't the strongest strap but it'll get the job done if any of these fuck niggas try you for a pussy." Rico never felt like he'd been threatened enough to want to kill someone, but he had been caught unawares in a shooting and nearly lost his life by a stray bullet. After that day, Rico started taking Silver with him everywhere he went. Just in case.

"Aye what's cracking, Rico? Do you like to be called that? You need a nick name. Rico ain't what I'd call swavy. What's your last name? Laman-e? Maybe I could come up with ..."

"Who is this?" Rico responded impatiently. He'd been asleep on one of his few nights off and had fully committed to getting some rest. An early morning phone call was unwelcome.

"Oh, my bad you sleep? This Jelz. Unc told me to come get you and take you around."

"Nigga it's 11. I just got out the club at 5. I'm really trying to chill but if we have business then I can get up but..."

"Great"

With that Rico could hear a knock on the door and noticed it also played through the phone. It was time to get up whether he liked it or not. As he pulled himself together, he realized who he'd been talking to. He wondered if Jelz knew anything about his father. It'd been months since he first started with the CABAL. Rico started to wonder if he was losing sight of the reason he was there. Was this his life now? What's the point in digging up old stories if he was happy? His father obviously didn't think that much about him since he was gone his whole life. So, should Rico waste all his time trying to learn about him? This was weighing heavily on Rico's mind as he got up and answered the door.

When he opened the door Jelz was there dressed like he was going to a skate park. A blue graphic tee shirt and dark tan cargo shorts with Vans sneakers.

Jelz noticed Rico was looking at him strangely. "Yo check this out.

Sick right?"Jelz said taking off his hat and handing it to Rico. It was a plain curved bill cloth hat with a small image of a photo realistic heart.

"I call it my mood display. The front has a heart now check out the back Barn! Broken heart."

Rico looked at the image on the back of the hat. Sure enough, there was the same heart but severed and stretched as if only held together by tendrils of blood. Rico thought the idea was clever but nothing to be woken up over. He opened the door and let Jelz into his place.

"Damn they gave you one of the remodeled joints. This is dope. Just like dad, right?"

Rico paused. "Why do you say that?"

"Well, I guess I didn't know it was a secret, but this used to be the Cat House. Used to be the nicest place here but now the building's been renovated so they're all nice. I've only been up here once or twice. It was Slick Cat's place. I figured that's why Mr. Prescott gave it to you."

Rico wasn't ready to handle the information being provided. Jelz seemed to be unbothered by the information he'd given so casually, even finding it amusing.

"You ever been here before...with Slick Cat I mean?"

"Yeah, I used to come though sometimes back in the day. I was an intern learning about engineering and sometimes I'd have to be a runner. Cat used to host meetings or invitation only parties here and once in a while I'd have to bring stuff."

"Like what kind of stuff" Rico asked intently.

"Cigars and stuff....my bad man. I heard he died not long-ago bro. I didn't know he had a son. I almost never saw him but when I did, he was chill. One of those guys that had a lot going on behind his eyes if you know what I mean."

Rico was curious, but his anger wouldn't allow him to see his father as anything less than someone that abandoned him. "Nah I don't. I never knew him. I never heard of him until I started working here."

"What?! That's crazy. This whole thing must be a mind fuck huh? Well man I'm sorry that happened to you bro. I can't imagine how that is but look at it like this: you're here now and it's yours. I didn't know the Slick Cat had a son. It almost makes him more human in a weird way. I don't know much about him. I was a kid. like 20 at the time. All I know is that he was the brains of this whole operation. When word came down that he died we didn't know what was going to happen. Mr. P was like a partner to him from what I could tell. I don't know who called the shots, but it had to be one of them."

Rico thought for a moment, "You seem to have a lot of information."

Jelz smiled, "Information is what I do and I'm here to show you how I do it. Mr. P stressed he wants you to know how things worked on the second level. Well, that's my level. I'm not Mr. Louis Vuitton and big rims like Money Mike. I'm on my own wave ya dig. Two things I'm good at making are connections and music. I can get anywhere I want if I need to."

"Sounds good," Rico said skeptically, audibly rolling his eyes.

"More than sounds bro. Think about it. I'm in your place and you don't even know how I got your phone or suite number."

Rico started to feel like the situation was once again out of his control

Was this guy a threat? Was he here to prove something? Rico approached him peering into his eyes. "Making it in isn't the same as making it out."

"Look man I'm not your enemy. Save the gangsta stuff for the gangsters. I'm cool with everybody. I heard how you handled things with Frxsh. I fucked with it so now I don't see a reason you and I can't be cool. Plus, don't you want to know more about the operation? The lounge ain't nothing but the face of all this. It's for networking and all that bravado shit. The CABAL doesn't end there. There's levels to this shit bro."

Rico couldn't help but like this guy. There was substance and knowledge behind the friendly personality. He also handled being threatened smoothly which told Rico this guy felt like he had nothing to hide that warranted any issues.

"So, what's the plan?"

"Well, I brought some stuff for you. I've seen you enough to guess your size. Now I know this isn't all that consumer-friendly mall merchandise you're probably used to wearing but trust me you're going to want to wear this." Jelz handed Rico a black bookbag with a smiley face pin.

Rico changed into a black tee with a large Japanese character on it and some white cargo shorts. Unwilling to compromise his shoes he threw on some black and white Reebok Kamikaze Shoes to match. After all, he had his standards. When he reached in the bag he found a wallet with a fake ID with his picture, a check card and $200 in 20-dollar bills. He walked back out to see Jelz standing where he left him.

"You could have sat down on the couch." Rico stated trying to remain stoic.

"Yeah man but this is your place. I like to respect people stuff. It's just how I was raised. I know how easily things can be taken the wrong way. My pops was a Gangsta Disciple from Toledo. He was a street nigga. I'm a creative, but I understood respect from a young age ya dig? I had to survive in the ATL before moving here to intern for Jason Class."

Rico paused. Jason Class was one of the premiere producers in Hip - Hop. He was considered an industry mogul. Rico never knew he once operated out of the CABAL. Jelz has been here five mins and dropped some big names Prescott, Mike, Slick Cat, and now J. Class. He also had a level of respect Rico understood. Maybe it was time to loosen up.

As they made their way to the sublevel parking, Rico tried to keep his mind off his father. Jelz obviously knew more than he let on but probably not enough to be considered a fountain of information on "Slick Cat". Rico thought the name sounded like a pimp or at least a player. The old names can be like that, and Rico only knew two men personally that would have info on a name like that: Mr. Prescott and JD assuming he's sober when Rico asks. Rico planned on asking soon. Before heading out Rico decided to message Adonis. Just in case.

/KEEP YOUR PHONE ON YOU/

/I GOT YOU/

"Who are you texting? Got you a lil baddie huh?" Jelz asked with his usual carefree tone.

"Something like that." Rico said, "Which car is yours?"

Jelz smiled. "Nothing crazy, just a Nissan. I bet you thought I was going to say a Charger or a Benz huh? Nah that's not my style. I like the simple things really. A to B type joint. There she is."

Jelz pointed to a car that looked like it should be on the cover of a video game. The Matte grey car was conservative, but its red accents demanded attention. In a fast and furious movie maybe, this car wouldn't stand out, but here in the CABAL it looked like it could outrun any car in the lot while still in neutral. Rico had never seen a Nissan like this.

Rico spoke up, "GTR, is that the name? I don't see these at the dealership."

Jelz laughed as they entered the car. "The dealership? Nah man I'm humble but I don't do what I do for nothing. I had the body made in Japan. I had some custom engine components put together in Europe and got it painted out in LA. But this is my favorite part. Check it out."

He pointed to his navigation screen. Rico looked to see what looked like a small yellow rabbit indicating the car's current position.

"It's Pikachu!! How fucking lit is that?!" Jelz said with so much enthusiasm he was almost yelling.

"Yeah, that's actually dope. How did you do that?"

"I know some guys that do some things with computers ya dig. Need me to hook you up?"

"I'm cool for now but that's dope still" Rico said, genuinely impressed. "So, where are we headed?"

"I have to go pick up some equipment and get some information for Mr. P. It shouldn't take long. We'll be back a few hours before the club opens. You working tonight?"

"Nah I'm off."

The ride was smooth. They drove through downtown talking about music and their favorite places to eat. Rico felt strangely comfortable around Jelz. He kept his guard up but felt almost foolish being so reserved. After a half hour, they arrived at a local lounge. It was too early in the day for the spot to be open, but the staff were setting up. Jelz told Rico to follow his lead. They stepped into a DJ booth where a heavy-set black man in his mid 20s was screwing with some wiring.

"Yo Liz what up bro. Lizard this my man Rico. Rico, Liz." Rico spoke up "What's up Li."

Before Rico could react Jelz had grabbed Lizard's head and smashed it into the sound board three times in cadence screaming "Where... the fuck... is my hard drive?!"

"I don't know? I must have misplaced it. Did you talk to Mike maybe he grabbed it ... or Frxsh you know how young niggas is," Lizard begged.

Jelz now had his arm around Lizard's throat. "Rico, Lizard can't remember how my hard drive went missing after his session last night in the studio. He thinks maybe Money Mike who doesn't have anything to do with music or Frxsh who I'm cool with might have it. How can we jog his memory?"

Rico never expected such an explosive fit of rage to come from someone with a personality like Jelz. Rico knew there had to be more to Jelz than his ability to handle music. He did say he was raised in Atlanta after all. Rico acted accordingly.

Putting silver to the man's cheek, Rico spoke in a low calm voice. "It's just a hard drive. They can be replaced just like teeth and flesh. I could remove all your wisdom teeth in one shot. Then we can trust what you say because we'll be able to see your lying tongue even when your mouth is closed."

Rico new he might be overplaying his hand, but he needed to establish himself as a martial force. The reputation of the CABAL depended on him being able to establish ruthless dominance when principal was on the line. Plus, a show of force might solidify the relationship between him and the only person that seems to know anything about his father.

"Ok ok I got it bruh. I didn't know it was yours. I just saw a free hard drive and figured it was empty. Bruh you ain't gotta shoot me. Here it's in my bag on the chair bruh real shit. I swear to god I haven't even plugged it in yet."

Rico had never seen a Lizard cry. He had a feeling he was about to.

"Oh sweet. Thanks Lizard," Jelz said instantly reverting to his usual tone.

He grabbed the whole bag. "Oh, and if you ever come back to the CABAL you'll probably never leave. I'd avoid that place for at least 6 months starting today. See you around bro."

With that, Jelz and Rico walked out the door.

twenty
nofrauds

"HOW DO YOU FEEL NOW?" Mr. Prescott sounded concerned but contemplative. "Have the drugs worn off yet, or are you still...struggling?"

Sienna looked up from her coffee, "I'm ok. I could have handled the situation, but they caught me off guard."

"We didn't expect the nurse to be a part of the operation. We're only glad you made it out alive. The question is what to tell our ... sponsors."

"We also need to find out who saved you and why she was there. Seems to me like some competition did show up. That ain't gon' work. We might have to see about that. If we had known there'd be so many moving parts, I would have gone with you." Mr. Fox spoke.

Sienna felt a twinge of relief through her shame at the botched mission.

Mr. Prescott spoke, "At any rate, that should help with the missing girls and keep the Fed out of our area of operation. Remember, we do a public service to our benefit. Do not let this distract you. You have a great track record, and Mr. Fox is an outstanding trainer. If he says it was unavoidable, I believe him. He was trained by the best."

Fox spoke to Sienna directly, "Even Cleopatra had bad days shawty. Get some rest for the next three days but watch your back. You never know if what that other hunter said is true or if she's been tailing you the whole time. Move normally but know I'll be close to you when you leave your house. Not to watch you but to watch out for you over the next week."

Sienna nodded her head in compliance. She knew she was getting off lightly. Mr. P had given her full pay plus a bonus. She was walking away with 6k for a botched mission. She had gotten good at what she did. Her name meant something in the world she travelled. Maybe not as big as Fox, but the Lady of the Nile was becoming more and more feared each day. Prescott helped make sure of that by spreading stories through his business connections at the CABAL. As Sienna approached the door, she looked over her shoulder.

"How is he doing?"

Prescott looked up from his desk, "Fine; he comes from good stock. More the pen than the sword, but he seems to be handling himself well. I feel like it's time for him to see more. I sent Mr. Jelz to keep him company today. Worried?"

"No. I know he's well protected." Sienna was hardly in the position to be making any kind of threat, but she let the idea hang in the air as she made her way out of the normal meeting place.

Sienna hated the idea of having competition. Learning the trade had changed her life up to this point. She'd found something special that she was good at. She knew her mother would understand, but she couldn't tell Rico. Not yet. The eventuality was starting to rear its head, and she realized she couldn't keep her secret forever.

Something that bothered her even more, was the idea that the mystery woman seemed to already know about her. At least the fact that Rico was her brother. Sienna had to wonder how common that knowledge was in the underground. The remark didn't seem personal or even like a threat, but more like a condescending dismissal. Sienna knew Prescott and Fox would investigate the situation, assuming they didn't set the entire thing up as a test She knew she'd have to do her own investigation, even though that wasn't exactly her forte. She was more skilled at wet work, not solving mysteries. Maybe it was time to talk to Rico. He's been at the CABAL so much that he lives there now. Sienna's still settling into her new condo refusing to admit she's still uncomfortable with the idea of leaving the house their mother left them. Rico's made a small reputation for himself at the lounge. He was invited to the table by Prescott himself. He's done well enough to maintain a certain elusive reputation, and now he's in a position others would kill for. That meant he was certainly being watched. Could he have made enemies?

"Type of games are being played; how's it going down..."

Sienna was nearly startled by her own phone. The last two days have had her on edge in a big way.

"Hello," she answered, knowing exactly who it was. She went through the normal prison phone call procedures.

"Aye shawty, what you got going?" Bolo responded on the other line.

His timing was perfectly off.

"I'm good, just coming home from work."

"Coming home? You work late, ain't it? Don't let me find out you out there on a pole shawty. I mean, get your money, but damn. I ain't even know you were doing all that."

Sienna couldn't tell if he was joking, "A pole? Are you serious right now? I do real estate work which means I have to meet clients at their convenience. I have to move like that when they want me to cause that pays my bills. I'm not on nobody's pole. Are you?"

Sienna knew the joke was over the line, but she didn't care. She was having a rough day and was not in the mood to be toyed with.

"What? These niggas know not to play with me. I got a pole all right. Soon as I came up in this muhfuka, I got me the Draco. I'm over here running shit, you hear me? They bring Bolo the big boy tray. They know I'm on that AMG shit. Yeah, yeah, all that."

Bolo's tone had gotten progressively louder and more tense as he spoke. Sienna has challenged his manhood. He gave his answer to her and anyone that was within shouting distance. She knew he was talking to her and at the same time accepting all challengers. Bolo was like that. Too aggressive for his own good. Sienna wanted to change the subject.

"Damn, lo, I get it. You don't have to do all that. You gonna create enemies."

"Man, I don't give no fucks bout these niggas. I be staying out the way, but these niggas know I'm a beast. They know I'm the whole thing. They know not to play with me. I call your phone to see if you straight, and you get to talking crazy on Bolo top. You are acting out of character, getting beside yourself."

Sienna knew she'd taken her frustrations out on Bolo and needed to reel him in. She had to think quickly.

"Bae, I'm sorry I was just a little shook up. I didn't mean it like that. I was out showing a client a new building out by the OB off 20."

Bolo interrupted, "The OB off 20 what's that?"

"You remember that time Nikki thought she was pregnant, but we didn't want to go to the clinic. Didn't you take us to that doctor's office on the north side? Over that way."

"Oh yeah, I know what you are talking about. What about it?"

"I was over there, and I saw a lady running out the clinic. She was dressed like a doctor, but I knew she wasn't. She looks like she just hit a lick or something. She slid out of there, and by the time I finished showing the building to my client, the police pulled up and started asking questions about somebody being killed in the clinic. The whole thing was crazy. I had to get out of there. I hate it cause I have to work over that area a lot. I don't want no psycho bitches running around making me look over my shoulder."

Bolo was quiet for a moment, "Shit, I mean the bitch hit a lick. Shit probably went bad, and I don't know. I can ask around and see if anybody know about some moves on the northside, but you gotta do something for me first."

"What's that?"

"Send me some pictures of Nikki. I wanna see what she look like now."

"Boy, don't get hung up on."

Bolo laughed, amused with himself, "I'm just playing, but damn a nigga can't get no picture, or nothing god damn."

"What kind of pictures you want, and don't even ask me to do what you are thinking."

"Shit, anything … can't show no fuckin'. Send me some shit that got these hoes bussin' it open showing some titties or something. That shit like money up in this muhfucka. I'm already getting money in this bitch, but I'm trying to build a lil empire. I don't want to run the dorm;

I want to run the whole wing out here. That's going to put me in these niggas pockets."

Sienna understood what she needed to do. The rest of the conversation was typical fare but enough for Sienna to get her mind off her most recent episode. She was thankful to hear Bolo's voice. He'd become a relief in her increasingly lonely world. She knew he'd look into what she asked simply because she asked. She just hoped that she'd left enough breadcrumbs for him to follow without compromising her own interest. She told herself that she would find him the sexiest freakiest pictures she could stomach when she got home. She wasn't getting on any camera, but she wanted to remind him she was still a lil nasty when she needed to be.

twenty-one
trappin' with the scammers

THERE'S a thin black line between the urban music industry and the prison system. The mass incarceration of minorities is magnified by the tales of those subject to institutional racism and generational poverty. Every day there are stories about black entertainers and athletes rising from these oppressive environments only to fall to the bane of America's most beneficial yet unwelcomed cultures. The source of this connection, of course, is the people. Lincoln-Way was full of residents that had some link to America's overflowing prison population. Everyone has a dad, brother, son, or ex-lover that was destined to spend untold years caged like animals. The question always came down to justice. Was there Justice? Well, it depended on who you asked.

There were always crimes, but the overarching circumstances of those crimes could rarely be captured in a single incident, a single headline, or a single investigation. The man who kills and steals and deals is rightfully condemned, but the environment that afforded no other opportunity is never altered. Middle and Upper-class America struggle to come to terms with the motivations of the street kids that roam the neighborhoods of Lincoln-Way. Money is the face of these motivations, and unfortunately, the face is all that is ever revealed to the world. The idea that greed is the root of all crime is as misplaced as the idea that sex is the root of all relationships. The root of the issue goes back as far as the slave trade. Suppose a house is only as strong as the foundation. The shaky infrastructure provided to once enslaved people can't be expected to stand strong in the same neighborhoods as the houses of those who would be their masters. The conservative might point to personal accountability. There's some merit in that. Suppose a boy is born into the lowest level of society. In that case, he's subject to poor education, slum lord living conditions, unbalanced opportunities, and the need to feel accepted by the community as a whole. There are some like Jelz and Frxsh that manage to navigate their way by excelling academically and being afforded opportunities as long as they are open to exploitation. There are some like Rico that strive to slowly work their way out by capitalizing on the little resources afforded to them by their environment. Men like Bolo often find themselves shepherded up into gangs like AMG. These organizations offer food, shelter, human interaction, and the opportunity to feel pseudo success in the face of economic failure. The plight of the people in this environment is expressed in their music. It started as negro spirituals, blues, jazz, rock and roll, and evolved (devolved?) into hip-hop. It's the sound of a struggle, and it's a song as old as time.

"Alright, alright, I see how you handled yourself, man. I appreciate you having my back," Jelz said, rousing Rico from his daydream.

"Yeah, man, I've been all over. I know how to handle myself for the most part." Rico replied for the first time, questioning if Jelz was safe...or sane.

As if reading Rico's thoughts, Jelz spoke again, "Look, man, I know shit gets crazy sometimes, but there's a metho...uh...what's the phrase again?"

"A method to the madness?"

"See what I did there? I got you to explain it to yourself. Ah-ha, gotcha." Jelz was just as jovial as he'd been when they left Rico's place earlier that day. Rico could see that there were many layers to Jelz, but he couldn't bring himself to dislike him despite the circumstances.

"Aight, what's next on the agenda?"

"Well, first, I'm hungry. Have you ever eaten Thai food? Shit's good. Don't look at me like that. I mean Thai food *is* good. I could go for some Pad Thai right now. Figured we might as well grab some lunch while we're out. There's a spot in River Town we can grab some. That also makes some bangin' Raman. I like to eat in Rivertown. Everybody just doing them, but at the same time, it feels like a community, you know? Makes me feel like I'm back in Atlanta chillin' on Edgewood."

Rico had been to Rivertown a few times but didn't know his way around. As they arrived, the streets seemed narrow and congested but very different from the rat race choked downtown districts. Rivertown was covered in Murals and dive bars that maintained just enough upkeep that anyone would feel comfortable in the informal environment. As they passed through, Rico could see people walking and laughing between establishments and street vendors. Every few feet, the music would change from Hard Core gangsta rap to Neo Soul to old school Marvin Gaye era R&B. Rico could tell this was a community that strove for peace and independence. A bar fight would get you thrown out, but shooting would get you excommunicated. The patrons and business owners were their own security, but police occasionally stopped in to watch the occasional open mic poetry slam or grab some cheesesteak egg rolls from a day bar. They were known by name and tolerated, understanding that they deal with any outsiders looking to cause trouble. The faint smell of beer and marijuana was on the breeze as a brown-Afroed woman painted a mural of MF Doom on the underside of an overpass.

"There was a spot there if you're looking for parking," Rico pointed out, hoping to end the casual ride and immerse himself in the bohemian scene.

"Nah, you sound like an out of towner. I know you been here before but passing through isn't the same as *being* here. Watch this."

Jelz drove behind a strip of the building where three middle-aged men more concerned about firewater than bathwater argued about who had the better football team in high school. Rico was shocked to recognize one of them.

"Man couldn't nobody stop the Dub ... hold on, is that my young fellow LW alumni Riki-Riki Rico?!" June Bug spoke as Rico and Jelz left the vehicle.

This time, Jelz was the one shocked. "You know JB? I guess you do come out of the ivory tower sometimes, huh," he laughed.

"Yeah, he's from my neighborhood," Rico confirmed.

"What?! Man me and Rico, go way on back, ain't that right Rico? Fellas, this a bad man, right here, the boy laser focused. One minute he is bagging groceries next he eating grey Poupon getting drove around like Scrooge McMoneybags."

"Yeah, alright, JB, we don't have much time. Here, watch the car. Imma grabs lunch. Make sure nothing happens, and I'll bring you back a beer."

June Bug stood at attention and gave a salute. "I will be your back ally sentinel, sir."

"Aight, if I see a scratch on the car, it's gonna be a scratch on your ass."

"My ass itch anyway," June Bug responded, causing the entire ally to erupt in laughter, including Jelz and Rico.

As they entered a small bar, they were greeted by alight-skinned woman with a boyish unlined Cesar haircut. Her freckled face said, "don't talk to me," but she smiled whenever she caught someone's attention.

"Hey Ken, I mean *Jelz* who's your friend?" Her voice was monotone, almost disinterested. Rico couldn't tell if she was friendly or not. She was hard to read already.

"Hey, Michelle, I mean *Shell*" Jelz playfully retorted. "This is my boy Rico. He works with me."

Shell turned towards Rico crossing her arms, "So you're one of the cultural zombies working for the city's legitimate crime syndicate posing as a lounge; it must be fun."

Rico wasn't sure where the hostility came from, but he could see there was a little compromise from this girl, and the gauntlet had been thrown. He wondered why she was so friendly to Jelz. Was there something there?

"Well, I just started there, so I'm more of a pilot episode. I guess it takes time to reach full syndication. How long did it take you, Jelz?" Rico stated without breaking eye contact with Shell.

"Man, my life is a movie, but the soundtrack is lit," Jelz said, amused with himself breaking the tension with sly laughter. "Anyway, I didn't know you were working today. I would have come by earlier to say what's up. My boy Rico's never been here before so try to be nice...If you can."

Rico could feel Shell's armor cracking, if only slightly. "Ok, Rico, I'm Shell. I've known Jelz for a long time. I'm just cautious of the company he keeps. He likes to take risk. I like to see him safe."

"Well, I wish him no harm. We're just grabbing lunch, and he told me this was the best spot to get it. I trusted him. Maybe you should too."

Shell smirked acknowledgement and proceeded to the DJ booth.

Confused, Rico spoke, "Hold up, she's the DJ? I thought she was the waitress."

"Nah, she's one of the 3 co-owners of the bar. She works on sound equipment by trade, but when she's here, she DJs sometimes. I met her back when I was learning to engineer. She's ... quirky, but ... you know how it is," Jelz said, still watching her spin.

Rico didn't need much of a clearer picture and decided to let it go for now.

"What would you like to eat?" a young male blasian waiter interrupted.

Rico spoke first, "Yes, I would like the Pad Thai with a Sweet tea, thank you."

Jelz erupted in laughter, "Pad Thai with a Sweet Tea", taking a sip from an invisible cup. "Why do you do everything so ... professional. Who do you think you are, James Bond? The President? You know what? That's what Imma is calling you, Mr President. Let me log that in my phone," Jelz said, pulling out his phone. "Oh yeah, let me get a number 2 extra sauce. Yall was skipping the sauce last time and a pineapple juice ... oh yeah, and whatever beer you like in a bottle, thanks.

The meal was brief, but Jelz kept the conversation engaging by constantly changing subjects. Rico enjoyed the atmosphere, but couldn't pull his mind away from what he'd learned about his father. Was he some successful playboy that didn't have time for a family? Was his family a dirty little secret, or was he protecting them? Rico decided that he'd better organize his thoughts once he was alone. Now was the time to learn about Jelz.

Walking back towards the car, Rico had to admire that Jelz kept to his word and brought June Bug a bottle of beer. Maybe supporting the habits of an addict wouldn't put them in a better position in life, but, for the moment, everyone was satisfied.

When they sat in the car, Jelz pulled out a bag of marijuana and a backwoods cigar. He unrolled the cigar removed the tobacco, and replaced it with the weed. "There's a trick to rolling woods. Everybody can't roll a good wood ya dig. You smoke?"

Rico had limited experience smoking weed. Sure, he'd smoke socially, but it never became a habit. He liked the prospect of selling more than smoking. In his younger teen years, he'd learned the values and measurements of weed distribution in the streets of Lincoln Way. He'd spent a few years doing small jobs for dope boys but never found it to be his calling. After flirting with the idea and losing some friends to "the life", he'd decided to pursue his income in a way that wouldn't take him from his mother and sister. Now he was with Jelz and decided to take a puff or two. The strong smell didn't come across as professional. Rico hated to be associated with guys that thought smelling like a pound of weed was a badge of honor. To him, it was a sign of immaturity. He rolled his window down, took two puffs and passed the blunt black to Jelz, who appeared to be tickled at the prospect of smoking with Rico.

"I honestly didn't think you smoked. You're full of surprises. Well, I have a surprise for you. Now it's time to show you how I operate." Jelz said with the first straight face Rico hadn't seen him wear in a while.

"What? Jelz...the in and out of jails part?" Rico asked, starting to feel the tension in his facial muscle relax.

"Yeah, when I have a message or question that needs to go through the system, I have to find my way into a jail cell but not in a way that will cause me longer than a 48-hour stay. There are 4 counties around here, and Rivertown is where they all meet. Being here gives me the chance to easily get to a different area and go to a different county. I can't do it too often, so I have to spread myself out. I used to do traffic accidents and bar fights, but that shit started adding up and threatening my license since it's tracked with the state. I need those L's, so now I've found a different way to go. Here take my keys and drive back to the CABAL. I'll call you once I'm back in pocket."

Rico was floored, "Just like that? You want me to take your car home and leave you out here to find a way to get arrested? Are you trippin'?"

Jelz continued to be uncharacteristically stoic, "Yes, this is a part of it. The CABAL is a network. I thought you knew that by now with all the time you spend with Money Mike. I used to engineer for Jay Class, but that reputation doesn't pay all the bills. I get sessions sometimes $100 per hour, 6 hours a day, 5 days a week. Other times it may be 2 weeks without a real dedicated artist paying for top-flight service. I had to find a better way to keep myself close to the music and the money without losing either. I was driving Uber to make ends meet until I picked up Mr. Prescott one day. I soon started hovering around the CABAL until I was a regular driver. One day Mr. P got in for a regular ride and asked me why I was so interested in driving him around. I gave him the breakdown. He said that he and his partner were thinking of adding a studio suite above the CABAL to keep the artist and dope boys close in case anyone blew up. He said his partner believed in legitimizing the business, which could be the first step. I knew I'd have to get my hands dirty as well. Well, one day, some AMGs got busted. Not just anyone though an "S class" named Pee Wee; the streets were all over the place. The violence had gotten bad. I'm sure you remember how hot it got about 5 years ago. Well, I had gotten into a fight with some pussy ass guy that couldn't handle his liquor. I spent a weekend in jail, and I knew who was next in line for the AMG. I put the word in Money Mike's ear, and the next thing I knew, I was part of the CABAL. Crazy, right?"

Rico had to admit the story was crazy, but it made sense. The CABAL seemed to be an anti-establishment that had dealings with all walks. Everyone knew the building held big secrets and dealt with the streets but the idea of going legit? Rico hadn't gotten the impression that was the organization's focus up to this point. This placed the CABAL in a different light. Rico had some thinking to do.

twenty-two
press

SIENNA DECIDED to find an apartment midtown. The environment was very superficial, but there was safety where the rent was high. She hated this thought process but knew for the time being that it was necessary to be in a new environment as she began trying to uncover the identity of her new rival. After her morning workout, she decided to take some time and cook herself a pancake breakfast. Even as a little girl, her mother used to tell her that she did her deepest thinking over a hot stove. For the first time in a while, her future felt uncertain, and some comfort food might be just what the doctor ordered. Today she'd relax and give herself time to rest and think. Tonight, was supposed to be an uneventful one, and she wanted to let her hair down and visit the CABAL. After her latest run-in with the new killer, she needed a drink, a tight dress, and a night off. The chance she'd see something she'd like among the urban riffraff posing as aristocrats were slim. She would, however, get a chance to see Rico running the show. She liked to see her brother work. He was a leader and could thrive in any environment. Cleo used her wilds to find the back door. Rico walked in the front door and convinced everyone the house was always his. Rico had charisma in spades; he just didn't fully understand how to use it yet.

As Sienna ate, she let her mind go back to her meeting with Fox and Mr. P, as well as her newly discovered rival. Mr. Prescott didn't seem to know much. That meant the competition was from out of town, or he was lying. She had to find out who would want to take credit for taking down a slimeball like the late Dr. Fowler. The problem was that there were plenty of people that would want to play the hero. The thought of playing hero never really occurred to her. Was she a hero? She always looked at her work as a necessary evil to help maintain the balance of power. She couldn't pay a visit to every corrupt business owner and politician because she'd have to nuke the US and large parts of Europe and Asia.

Mr. Prescott was a difficult character for Sienna to wrap her mind around. He came across as classy and mild-mannered, dressed in business suits and wore expensive cologne meant to be underwhelming by design. Mr. Prescott did a good job of making Sienna feel like she was an important part of keeping the city safe without the confines of due process. Even in situations like the dentist office incident, he would meet with her face to face.

Sienna doubted that he met with his public staff that often. Was she being manipulated? She simply couldn't see how. Most of her targets were threats to society, not necessarily the CABAL itself or any of Mr Prescott's other interests. Sienna decided to continue to trust Mr. Prescott for now. Time will reveal any current deceptions, and she's getting pretty good with a blade.

A phone call interrupted her thoughts.

"What's up, CC," Rico spoke on the other end. "I came by the house today to see if things were going smoothly with your move, but it looks like you got it knocked out."

"Yeah, the moving company finished early. I spared no expense," she said jokingly.

"Spared no expense; you sound like a midtown girl already."

"I mean shit; you know what the fuck going on? I slid out that bit on my momma I was ridin.'"

Rico burst out laughing. "Now, you sound like a girl from the Dub."

Sienna always liked to hear her brother laugh. It was a reminder of lost days and long summers. It was a reminder of simpler times, of their mother letting them lick the cake batter from the mixing bowl. It was

Dragon ball Z and the Proud Family. It was the home she could never return to but would never forget.

"Well, I can tell you it wasn't easy, but I'm glad I'm here now. Have you thought about what I said about renting it out? It would be a nice rental property. Mom would be jumping for joy to hear us talking about rental property and all that."

"Yeah," Rico responded, "I'd say an Airbnb but don't nobody wanna visit the city and stay in the hood. Isn't Laura a real estate agent? Why don't you ask her about getting tenants? I'm sure two more kids out there could use a home. Besides, I don't have a problem coming by and checking on the place. My busiest time is at night anyway."

Sienna had to admit that it was a good idea, "Yeah, ok, that sounds good. I'll hit her up and ask. Are you working tonight? I was thinking about pulling up, so keep the gold teeth and worn-out polo shirts at bay if you can. I might come from the Dub, but I can do better than that, I think."

"Oh shit. Imma have to grab a new shirt and a toothbrush for Money Mike. Nah, I'm kidding. It's not like that. Mike and I have streamlined the place. It's his formula; I just adopted it. The city is full of people with money. Outside the CABAL, that money is separated by community lines. The Lounge is where the 200k a year engineer can break bread with the 200k a year coke boy. Kind of eliminates the need for extortion, and hopefully, we can get some unity between worlds instead of gentrification. That might be a reach, but hell, it's a start."

"The idea sounds good; just make sure you don't fall too far on one side or another. Power and money can mess your spirit up and put you in bad situations. I'd hate to be up in there raising hell bout you. You know I'm low key ratchet." Sienna replied using her best Cardi B impression.

"Yeah, I know. I'm being careful. I'll tell you what, why don't you send me your address and I'll have someone pick you and whoever you want up at 9? Food's on me. Drinks on you. I wonder if Asia is free tonight," Rico mused.

"Boy, Asia is NOT coming, so don't even think about it, but that sounds dope. I appreciate you, bro."

"Hey, what are brothers for."

After the phone call, Sienna decided she had just enough time to head out to the practice range to work on her long-range accuracy, and maybe stop by Macy's and pick up a cute dress.

After a long evening of shooting, shopping and cleaning, Sienna was finally able to look at herself in the mirror. Nicole was sweet enough to do her hair and do it she did. Sienna's natural curls had been straightened into long thick waves with amber highlights. She decided to spoil herself with a low cut deep green dress that showed just enough cleavage and thigh to be attractive but non-approachable. Green and Gold pumps that looked like they came from Italy matched the accessories in a way that made her feel more like Cleopatra than even the cleanest freshly oiled .50 cal. Sienna always did her makeup. Mom taught her how to keep her cheeks rosy, but her longtime friend Claudy taught her how to contour her face into that of a goddess. Sienna was applying a maroon lip when her doorbell rang.

When she opened the door, the girls were in full effect. Nicole had a black and white wide striped dress with killer black heels. Laura wore a Maroon leather one-piece pants suit that Sienna fully planned on borrowing at some point. Asia wore a deep navy sleeveless evening dress with exposed hips missing nothing but somebody's son's teeth marks and knee-high black boots.

Nicole spoke up first, "Bitch, we looking like Destiny's Child made a comeback. I hate to steal the shine from the center stage, but I mean damn, we have a whole vibe."

The girls spent the next 5 minutes complimenting each other and exchanging fashion tips and gossip before Sienna received a text telling her the car had arrived. When the ladies got downstairs, Sienna recognized the white Range Rover as one from the CABAL. As if reading her thoughts, Adonis stepped out and opened the door for the ladies. Sienna took a step towards the passenger seat until she felt a sharp kick, and Nicole stepped past her quickly, giving her a look that said, "back off, he's mine." Sienna couldn't help but shake her head and laugh at her friend. "Go get him girl is all she could think as the whole crew headed out into the night.

twenty-three
man of the year

"AYE, don't let them young niggas in yet. They gonna scare off all the women, man." The lounge was in rare form, and Money Mike was in full director mode. "Aye Rico, make sure the 3rd booth gets 3 bottles of Bumbu Creme. They do not drink white or brown, and we want them to feel comfortable. Nah, a matter of fact, you go with him." He said, pointing to one of the new greeter girls. "Yeah, that'll work. I heard the guest likes long legs. Go in there, give him his shit but don't give him any play. We in the look but don't touch industry. Being untouchable keeps our value high. Go in there and act too good for those rich boys."

Rico and the girl did as they were asked. Rico liked to see Mike in this mode. He and Money Mike had become sort of a Batman and Robin duo at the Lounge, and people seemed to feed off their chemistry.

"Aye, Rico," Adonis said as he approached. "There's like three young niggas outside trying to get in. They look like rappers or some shit. I'm not feeling their vibe, so I deaded the whole situation and told them I'd see."

Rico thought for a minute, "Nah, Mike wants to keep the crowd cool tonight. We got Anderson Paak hitting the stage, so we want to keep the atmosphere jazzy. Tell you what, give them a free table pass for the Young Thug show tomorrow night with our apologies. Blame it on me if they trip."

"Aight bet," Adonis said, moving smartly.

Adonis was becoming more and more a part of the lounge staff. His days driving would be over very soon if Rico had anything to say about it. Rico decided that if things went well tonight, he asked Mike about rotating Adonis in the lounge in his place as he spent more time dealing with Jelz and the studio suites.

Rico headed up to bring the bottles with his wait staff. He liked to make sure he was seen working at all levels. It kept him informed of personnel movements and the flow of the business throughout the night. When he got to box three, he saw a group of three. There were two white men and one black woman.

"Ms. Reichertz," one man spoke in a distinctly British accent, "I believe you'll find a partnership with our brand to be lucrative on an international level. We've been working and building our brand in the US, and we see such great potential."

The woman they spoke to was tall, dark, and moved like a model. Rico once recognized her as Yasmine Reichertz an, on the rise, interior designer of the stars known for mixing Panafrican styling with German pragmaticism. Her designs and radical ideas had began to take shape in the world of couture fashion placing her firmly in the running for the next big thing in the European fashion houses. She was listening but appeared unmoved by the plea.

"Gentleman, my designs are about more than the bottom line. My garments carry the spirits of the designer. I'm inspired by people and want to bring them together. That is my goal, and I'm sure to make it happen. I don't see the point of flooding the US market with my brand because it will hurt my exclusivity. I can't allow myself to be too accessible. Wouldn't you agree,

Mister...?"

"Rico," Rico spoke up as drinks were presented and poured.

"Mr. Rico, you look like a man that understands consumer demands. What do you think about opening the doors of this establishment to the general public without vetting your patrons?"

Rico thought for a moment he knew he had to measure his words because people like Ms. Reichertz were rarely seen so publicly the CABAL could always stand to receive a boost in reputation especially among the visiting wealthy elite, "Well, I'd say that while our name would be more commonly spoken, our value would diminish. Our client base would change, and the principles the CABAL was built on would risk misrepresentation."

Ms. Reichertz smiled, "Exactly my point sweety, thank you. My brand is about representation across all regions and colors. We look to express the beauty of the world. How can we do that if we associate with a marketing firm that employs less than 3 percent minorities."

Rico saw the men's faces go white. "Ms. Reichertz, I assure you we're making every effort to make our team as inclusive as possible."

"Yes, I'm sure, but...thank you, Mr. Rico. It's good to patronize an establishment that understands the value of representation. I'll remember that." Rico and the waitress began to exit when Ms. Reichertz locked eyes with the waitress.

"And I would like to know your name too. If you bring me a bottle of your favorite drink alone...maybe you can tell it to me," Ms. Reichertz gave a sly yet seductive smile. She was a hunter.

Rico headed downstairs to check the sound. Anderson Paak would arrive very soon, and Rico wasn't sure which sound man was scheduled to take care of the system. He could see someone working under the equipment and heard a voice he could never have expected.

"What up, man. This shit about litty. Aye Paak got some heat. You are going to be able to feel the vibe in your skin when these vocals hit the air." Jelz said, stepping out. After noticing the surprised expression on Rico's face he let out a confused. "What?"

"Well, I mean...damn, you got out fast," were all the words Rico could muster through his astonishment.

"I told you this is what I do, bro," he pats Rico on the arm. "You'll get used to it. I also asked about any info on your pops. There's no guarantee anything will come up, but we'll see."

"I appreciate that bruh," Rico said, humbled by the kindness. Jelz was hard to dislike and Rico had given up on trying. "Well, let me make sure things are going well close to the stage."

Rico couldn't stay for long. The building was filled with faces old and new. The Lounge was in rare form, but it was nothing Rico couldn't handle. Rico liked when things were moving at a fast pace. He could feel the importance of his role at the lounge. Every face he greeted, every hand he shook, every fire put out was further proof that he belonged. This was his new comfort zone. Here he was appreciated, and his reputation was solid. He knew his mom would be proud, but there was a more pressing matter: He hadn't checked on his sister.

Heading to the stage front tables, Rico could see Sienna, Nikki, and Laura eating shrimp cocktails and looking like a bouquet of black beauty. Sienna was just a dolled-up version of the same little tomboy she always had been, but the other two ladies stepped it up for the night.

"Feels like something's missing, doesn't it," words stopped Rico a few yards from his sister's table. He turned around to find Asia staring at him with 2 drinks in hand. Rico already knew Asia could make herself irresistible, but tonight she was out to turn heads and break hearts. The code word was sexy without gratuity or overexposure. Few women could show off a coke bottle without looking thirsty themselves. Asia was one of the few.

"I'm surprised you're here. I didn't think you went out much. Welcome to the Cesar and Brutus Alliance Lounge." Rico spoke, trying to sound as professional as possible.

"Well, no, I don't move around that much, but neither does CC. Soon as I heard, she wanted to go out ... and to the CABAL of all places ...! had to make it happen."

Rico felt his professionalism weakening and his flirtatious instincts taking over. "Now that you're here, what will you do ... being a fish out of water and all?"

"Well, maybe I'll find a handsome sailor to swim with. I wonder who here has a boat?" Asia responded in kind, ready for the verbal volley.

"The view is probably better from the crow's nest," Rico nodding up at the skybox booths. If Asia was looking for a rich sucker, she could probably have anyone up there. Rico was sure by now quite a few trust fund kids and gold toothed rappers had their eye on her.

"Well, those are for birds. I prefer the view from here." She said, handing Rico a drink. "Mr. Mike sent a bottle to the table courtesy of the house. I thought maybe you could use a drink too. Since the house is buying and all." Rico looked around and saw Mike and Adonis talking by the entrance.

Mike looked over and gave Rico the "I put you in position" smile that guys give each other when they're trying to facilitate an opportunity for sex for a friend. Money Mike was flashy but still a hell of a wingman. Adonis was looking as well, trying to hide his laughter. Rico felt like he was at an upscale high school dance.

"I'll have to talk to them about that one. Thanks for the drink. I'll have to keep it as long as I can. Wouldn't want your efforts to go to waste. You know what they say about that. Waste not ..." Rico casually placed his hand on Asia dress on the exposed section of her hip. "... want more"

"We'll see..." were Asia last words before walking back to her table with a walk that told Rico she anticipated his lingering look.

Just as quickly as the moment had presented itself, it was over. The reality check came in the form of Frxsh and his entourage. Rico could see that there had been a problem. Frxsh was with Macktown and Big Steps local rappers that were here to make it known they were the new big artist in town. Rico knew Macktown from the dub he was a gaudy ghetto fabulous type. Big rims on yellow and black cars. He was a true southern rapper but he always came across as friendly and non-judgmental. Big Steps was from the country. He was a short hefty nearly 300 lbs rapper with the cool casual demeanor of a BIG or Rick Ross. Rico only knew him by reputation. Frxsh wasn't the type to bring trouble. He had the mischievousness of any 22 year old local celebrity, but he was a humble guy at heart. Whatever had just occurred had the whole crew mad, and when crews with reputations get mad, lives are in danger. Money Mike usually handled the street warfare. He was close to PJ and a few AMG OG's from 10 years ago. That meant he was a real factor between war and peace. Mil<:e was up in the lounge talking to the Skybox guest. Rico could see Wiz and two girls in the booth. Mike and Wiz looked to be in a heated argument. Rico knew by now that it meant they were talking sports. He'd have to be the one to deal with the ruckus.

"Yo Frxsh, what up with you. Y'all boys came to chill, right" Rico asked as friendly as he could muster.

"Aye Rico bruh, these LAME ass niggas out here playing with my top."

Macktown chimed in, "Fa real they are gone make me take off on they stupid ass."

"On God these niggas some ants. They must not know we Big BenI' Big Step cosigned creating a BB hand sign.

Rico could see there was something wrong but nothing he couldn't handle. Looked like Big Step was AMG which meant while he would normally be one to watch, he would respect Money Mike and, by proxy, Rico, if only temporarily. He was working...no, he was the CABAL as far as the world could tell, and he had to act accordingly.

"Alright, tell you what. Where are y'all sitting? Let's get you guys seated l to help you better enjoy the night. Niggas on the outside don't matter; that's why they are out there, and you're in here. You matter here. You're a guest of the CABAL."

Frxsh struggled to maintain his anger at the offer of the celebrity treatment.

"I mean shit; you know how I'm coming. I'm paid for an up-close table ya feel me. Can't be fresh on the outside tables..but I mean cut a nigga a deal on a bottle we'll each grab one."

"No deal," Rico said with a deadpan face. He let it linger. "I mean damn Rico, I thought we were cool, I guess-"

"There's no tab on your first 2 bottles in the Skybox. You gotta pay full price for the third."

Frxsh smiled bigger than Rico had ever seen. Big Step started stroking his chin in approval mumbling the words "Ok, ok" to himself. Macktown spoke up

"Oh shit, I'm fuma what? Turn up in the bitch!"

Rico got the reaction he wanted. He led the guys to the last Skybox. Once they were seated, he spoke.

"Alright, guys Me and Mike each have our boxes to use when the place is too full or in case of an emergency. I'm letting y'all have this one for tonight because I fuck with Frxsh. As long as y'all don't fuck my shit up or fuck the night up for anybody consider it an upgrade for the night."

"Can we smoke in here?" Macktown asked. "Hell Nah, you know that," Frxsh corrected.

"Don't worry about it. I'll send up some Ciroc and a menu."

"You ain't gotta do that, bruh." Big Step spoke up, "We appreciate you, but we ain't probably gon' eat too much. A nigga just really came to chill, maybe snatch up one of these boogie hoes, you feel me. Some niggas was outside looking all hard and shit. Macktown asked a nigga for a lighter, but niggas was acting tough. I started to step down on one of them niggas, but I just was like fuck them niggas. They broke."

Frxsh spoke next, "Hell yeah, plus PJ said anybody gets to shooting out here where his brother be at then it's an automatic green light on whoever do it. Fuck all that. Them niggas ain't crazy."

Rico laughed, "Yeah, you know how it goes. They probably outside waiting on whatever boogie hoes y'all turn down."

This got a laugh out of everybody. Rico had hit his stride. In one fell swoop he'd strengthened the CABAL's reputation with the future of the AMG and local hustlers. Mike had an in with the OGs but Rico was building a relationship with the new breed. As he began to exit the booth he stopped and turned.

"By the way, the secret menu is only for the CABAL's special guest. Any vice you have, we can provide it. You can't smoke, but we have top of the line vapes, shrooms, edibles, tabs, pills, spikes, and powders. I'll send a girl up."

As Rico stepped out of the booth and headed towards the stairs, he heard familiar laughter coming from Ms. Reichertz booth.

"... I didn't know whether to slap her or take her to a hospital. Girl, it was something else ..."

It couldn't have been who he thought it was. Rico decided to step in. "Ms Reichertz, I wanted ..." Rico stopped mid-sentence. Sitting across from Yasmin Reichertz, the upcoming fashion guru was Alanna.

"Ooooh, the night gets interesting. Hi Rico. I like that outfit on you. Have you met Yas Reichertz?"

Yasmin spoke, "Yes, me and Mr. Rico spoke earlier. I like him. We're slowly becoming acquainted."

Rico never broke eye contact with his on and off fling, "Yes, we met; how do you know her?"

"Well, I ran into her crew as I entered the building. I came here looking for some excitement; instead,I'm over here trading stories with a legend. The CABAL: Bringing people together."

"Ok, I'll let you ladies have it. Ms. Reichertz, is there anything else you need?"

"No, sweety, thank you. I've fallin' in love with this little empire you guys have here. I'll tell you what. Here's my card. If you ever need me. I'll call you."

Rico hesitated at the last statement but understood Yas was influential enough to get in touch with anyone she wanted. He looked over at Alanna. She bit her lip and gave him a wink that would have crippled a weaker man.

"Girl, you're going to make him blush."

"I like it when he blushes."

"Okay, well, that's my cue, ladies. Enjoy your night," Rico left quickly because everyone in the room could see him sweating under the collar. Asia was an interesting prospect, but Alanna was a hellcat that knew how to control a room in or out of bed.

The show went off without a hitch. Anderson Paak's rhythmic poetry had the crowd eating out of his hand. His smooth vocals and unpredictable wordplay were too highbrow for the dub, but here in the CABAL, it was mana from heaven, and the people were eating their fill. Halfway through the show, he brought out Schoolboy Q, and all the dope boys in the house gave universal approval rarely seen among the gangsters. A blending of cultures and classes defined the Cezar and Brutus Alliance Lounge. The air was cool; the staff were busy. The guest was happy.

Rico took the time to survey the room. Adonis was at the bar talking to Nicole. Wiz had come down from his booth to see Schoolboy Q. He and Mike were no doubt talking about music.

Jelz took Nicole's seat and had Sienna and Laura cracking up with another guy Rico didn't recognize. Everyone seemed to be enjoying the night Rico knew he'd made two distinctly important connections tonight: Yasmine and Big Step. Yasmine was above board and had the corporate influence to dwarf a place like the CABAL. Big Step was an AMG, and the way he moved, he was at least an E class. He looked about the same age as Sienna's ex boyfriend Bolo, but something about him was more conservative, almost wise. Rico had locked in the legit and the illegal in one night. Money Mike would be proud.

As the stage cleared, Rico was surprised to see the cool sophisticated walk of Mr. Prescott. He walked up to the microphone like he was about to serenade the audience. He spoke to the crowd thanking them for their patronage and gave a short, poignant speech about preserving culture and community. In the end, he addressed Rico directly.

"...Lastly, I want to take a brief moment to acknowledge a face that is no longer new to the lounge. I brought this young man aboard and told him he had what it took to carry on the spirit here. In the time he's been a part of our family, he has proven he can be a trusted asset and help carry the torch for the lounge and the culture. Everybody raise a glass to our newest member Mr. Rico Lamarre."

There were raised glasses in every hand. Rico felt the world spinning around him. Sienna was glowing with pride. All the people he'd met were there showing him love. Even Frxsh and his crew were holding up bottles in his honor. Rico had arrived.

twenty-four
bad and bougie

PULLING up to the CABAL as a guest felt so strange to Sienna. Not that she was complaining. Being picked up and delivered like a prize to the world was a feeling she could get used to. Asia and Laura were talking about everything from hair to Bitcoin trading. Nikki was upfront making moves on Adonis. Everyone was looking and feeling like a Diva. When the crew arrived, Adonis dropped the ladies off and let them "red carpet" walk to the lounge entrance. There was a line, but apparently, the ladies were exempt. Sienna noticed a few guys that didn't seem too happy with the line arguing with some local rappers one of which she recognized as Frxsh. She didn't have time for that. It was time to be a Queen. Sorry guys. Asia was all smiles. Laura moved like she owned the place, and Nicole kept repeating the phrase "as it should be" every chance she got. It was one of those moments you can never understand if you've never wielded black girl magic.

As they entered the CABAL, they were greeted by a tall, dark man wearing clothing brands they mostly saw in music videos. Sienna had the suspicion this was Money Mike.

"Yall looking like somebody ordered y'all off a menu," he complimented as he walked them to their table.

"Ok, ladies, Adonis messaged me and told me you all didn't want a booth, so I put you upfront center stage. Best seats in this muthafucka.

You'll be able to tell me what kind of cologne Anderson wore tonight. Now, which one of you is Sierra?"

"I'm *Sienna.*"

"Oh, my bad, I tried to memorize it. Rico told me his sister was pulling up with her friends, but he didn't tell me *all* yall was fine. Well, shit, let me introduce myself. I'm Mikel. Everybody calls me Money Mike. There are two things I know how to make: Money appear and good looking women happy. You guys got top billing. Drinks on the house as long as you don't throw up. You get to doing that; Adonis or Jelz may have to drop yo ass off at the crib. It'll still be in style, though."

Everyone laughed presently. Sienna could tell that the gentleman that was speaking to them; this "Money Mike" was not used to being so polite and gracious. It made Sienna wonder what Rico had done to earn this kind of treatment for his guest. She hoped it wasn't anything dangerous. Mike was a sweet guy, but there was dirt under his nails, and she could feel it. He seemed like someone that was better a friend than an enemy. She could read his body language and accent to determine that his customer service voice was consistently filtered through street slang. She didn't mind though. After all, everyone has their secrets.

As the night moved on, Sienna could see Rico strategically moving from one lounge section to the other. He had become a maestro, and the entire place seemed to move to the beat of his drum. Sienna was proud to see her brother working in such a professional manner. She knew their mom would too. Asia excused herself just as two men approached the table. As if on cue, Nikki started disinterestedly sorting through her phone, and Laura stared daggers into the as-of-now unwelcome guest.

"Hey, what's up? My name's Jelz. Are you guys enjoying your night?"

Sienna didn't want to acknowledge the man, but his innocence and incorruptible charm were inescapable. Sienna contemplated a response, then the unexpected happened. Laura replied flatly.

"Yes, we are. What about you guys?" Sienna knew the night was special Laura was hardly friendly but even she couldn't escape the vibe of the evening.

"I'm chilling; it's cool. I work mostly at night, but I usually stick around for the show. This is my guy Jay Class. I used to intern with him back in the day."

"Well, I'm Laura. This is Nikki, Sienna, and damn, I forgot Asia went to the bathroom, I think." Each lady gave a brief greeting. "Can I ask you a personal question?"

The tension in the air had started to thicken. What did these men want?

They hadn't made any moves, but they talked to the girls like they were old friends. Even Nicole was paying attention now.

Laura thought for a moment, "Sure, why not? What's up?"

"Well, I've been on my 'loc journey for like 2 years now. I see your style, but they look so soft and ...well, like they glow. What do you put in your hair?"

The table erupted with laughter. No one expected Mr. Jelz to ask about hair care. Sienna was enjoying her newfound company. Mr. Jelz kept the ladies in stitches. Mr. Mike was true to his word. Sienna saw even found herself thinking how cute Mr. Class was looking. She'd have to take time to decide if he was cute *enough*. Drinks were flowing, and the show was starting nicely. Asia had returned to the table after some time, looking like she'd gotten away with murder. Sienna knew it was only a matter of time before she made a move on Rico. She didn't really have a problem with it. She found it almost adorable.

Anderson Paak's show was surprisingly captivating. Sienna had the feeling he was looking at her the whole time he was performing, but she couldn't be sure because he wore dark circular sunglasses that made it impossible to tell. Sienna wasn't the type to care about celebrities, but a man that could sing was one of the most disarming things in the world. She decided to let go and just get lost in the mood.

Once the performance was over, Sienna was shocked to see Mr. Prescott grace the stage. He was normally very reclusive, and business minded. Sienna was still sore about her mission involving Rico, but now wasn't the time. Mr. Prescott gave a short speech and congratulated her brother for his accomplishments at the CABAL. Sienna was swept up in the words and seeing the most exclusive establishment shower praise on her brother filled her with pride. As she looked around the room, she noticed the center Skybox. It was larger than the rest by a small margin, and you could see non-detailed silhouettes that didn't appear to be looking at Rico...they appeared to be looking directly at her..or was it, Mr. Prescott? Sienna couldn't tell. Maybe she was paranoid after the incident at Dr. Fowlers and saw shadows in the dark.

As the night became the morning, Nikki and Adonis approached the table. She spoke, "Well, you all are ready to call it a night? You know I got church in the morning."

"Girl, you ain't got no church," Sienna quipped as the girls all took turns teasing each other. Adonis walked all the ladies to the door. Just like when they arrived, the Range Rover was parked front and center. Anderson and Schoolboy were being escorted out with security and quickly signing autographs along the way.

POP POP POP POP POPPOPPOP

That was all it took. The entire event was frozen in time as smiles and intoxication turned into mortal terror. Being in a crowd during a shooting always feels like a guessing game. People were screaming and scrambling in all directions, including the shooter. That was the difference between Sienna and her girls. They might have become entrepreneurs, creatives, and the like, but they were still from Lincoln Way. Nicole ran and ducked behind the truck for protection. Laura grabbed Sienna and squatted next to Nicole. Through the crowd, Sienna could hear more gunshots as Adonis tried to usher the girls into the car, telling them that it's an armored vehicle designed for Mr. Prescott. Sienna was happy to be safe until one thought crossed her mind.

Rico.

It took 5 seconds for the street-savvy ladies to crowd into the vehicle. Adonis reached in the glove compartment and grabbed a black pistol that Sienna recognized as a Glock 40. He layed it on the seat and reached back to grab Nicole. As everyone was panicking, Sienna snatched the pistol off the seat and took off into the crowd. She had to make sure her brother was safe. If he wasn't, someone was about to die.

twenty-five
once again, its on

THE NIGHT WAS ALMOST OVER. Rico and Jelz were standing outside the entrance. Mike talked to Mr. Prescott and watched as the streets filled with high-end shoes and heels. The night had been a success. The staff were free to leave as they chose once the place was back in order.

"Rico, Jelz, let me talk to you." Mr. Prescott spoke in a surprisingly jovial tone. As they approached, Rico could see the crowd beginning to part. Rico grabbed Jelz.

"Aye isn't that..." was all he could get out before Lizard and two other men opened fire at him and Jelz. Rico realized these were likely the men Frxsh and his entourage had mentioned earlier. There was a mad scramble as shots rang. Rico grabbed Silver from his waistline and began blindly firing back, silently praying he didn't hit anyone in the crowd. The .380 was out of bullets in seconds flat as the men began to rush back into the safety of the building Rico, starting hearing shots from two other directions.

POP-POP

Rico saw Lizard hit the ground. As his eyes followed the sound, he couldn't believe what he saw. Sienna was crouched behind a car holding a black pistol like an FBI agent protecting the president. When did she get a gun? When did she learn to shoot?

POPPOPPOP

Zip Zip

Rico could hear bullets shooting past him. He was exposed; he couldn't figure out who had shot the additional shots, but Lizard was down, and his crew had run. Sienna was already closing the door of the Range about to take off. There was nothing to do but slam the doors of the CABAL shut.

"Bro wtf wtf," was all Jelz could say as he grabbed Rico. "The fuck you standing in the doorway for!! Nigga damn. Are you ok?"

The reality of what had just happened was beginning to dawn on Rico.

Someone was shooting at him and Jelz. Jelz had roughed Lizard up and Rico had threatened him, but he hadn't put his life in danger. Could they want revenge that bad for a retrieved hard drive?

"Bro, was that fucking Lizard out there shooting at us?! I'm killing that muthafucka!" Jelz was enraged.

"Hey, we need a hospital NOW, gentlemen. Stop sitting on your hands and call the damn ambulance."

Rico turned to see a visibly stressed Prescott kneeling over Money Mike.

Jelz was already dialing. Rico ran over.

"Mike, oh shit, man Jelz is calling the folks they'll be here in a minute, man."

Money Mike spoke, "Damn nigga they hit me in the fucking leg. Shhh Aghh FUCK this shit burning like a muthafucka."

"Alright, they are on the way, bro; try to stop the bleeding and stay focused. Imm a get you some water or something," Jelz said frantically.

Rico was in a panic but trying to remain calm. He ran behind the bar, grabbed two cloth napkins, and tied them together to form a makeshift tourniquet.

"Aye, bruh, I think that's it, bruh" Mike's voice was getting louder weaker and weaker.

"Don't worry about it. I took a class on this at Food Shark. We gotta slow the bleeding down till the folks get here."

As Mr. Prescott held Mike up, occasionally wiping his head, he assured him that he was safe and that he would scorch the earth to find out who did this. Blood had soaked Mikes pants, and then a puddle was forming on the floor. Rico was desperately trying to tighten the tourniquet with all his strength. Mike reached up and grabbed Rico's hand with a knowing look.

"Say bruh, don't worry about that. I'm straight. I'm tired as fuck, and I can't even barely feel that shit. Anymore say bruh."

A large kick to the door threw it open, revealing Wiz, Frxsh, Big Step and Macktown.

Rico recognized Wiz had one of Lizard's crew in a choke hold and bleeding from the mouth. Macktown had blood on his chest and hands, painting a clear picture of why Lizard's friend was so bloody.

Big Step kneeled beside Mike, "Damn OG, we smoked one of them niggas and Macktown grabbed the other one. Damn, he ain't looking good, bruh. Is that shit working?

"I'm doing my best, bruh," Rico snapped, frustrated.

Wiz approached his friend. Rico could see the pain in his face. Once he saw the blood, a single tear streamed from his red eyes. He sat down beside Mike and grabbed his arm.

"Bruh, this shit for life. I not gonna let you be by yourself." With that, he stuck two cigarettes in his mouth and lit them both.

Mike was starting to cough blood. He briefly stopped to inhale the cigarette Wiz was now holding up to his lips. His baby blue shirt was now speckled with wine droplets that told a story no one but Wiz seemed ready to accept.

Rico felt Frxsh's hand on his shoulder. Mike was gone.

Death was a part of life in Lincoln-Way, but Rico couldn't imagine something like this happening at the lounge. The deafening silence was almost too much for Rico to handle. A deep rage touched Rico that he hadn't felt in himself in a long time: Rage and Sadness.

"Bring him ... to me," the grisly words of Mr. Prescott broke the void of nearly empty sound that had filled the room. The unfamiliar and oppressive sound shook Rico to his core. This situation was far from over. The CABAL, a sacred pillar of urban culture and ingenuity, had been violently thrust into darkness. Rico was still wrapping his mind around the fact that he would never hear Mikes booming voice or infectious sense of humor again. The balance that he'd brought to the lounge couldn't be overstated. This was a death the entire city would feel. There would be a mass exodus of the legitimate business partners the CABAL had hosted due to a fear of being associated with street violence. On the other side, Rico knew there'd be war. No one had to say it. Money and Death always brought war. Rico could remember how hard the AMG boys had to fight to take over the local drug trade. Those days were some of the worst Lincoln Way had seen. Luckily, the drug trafficking revolution yielded some stability. Now everyone in the streets would be claiming to have a part of tonight or trying to figure out how to capitalize on the wanton violence.

Rico watched as Macktown and Big Step drug the beaten man closer to Mr. Prescott. Or at least the man that appeared to be Prescott. Rico wasn't sure anymore. Mr. Prescott was still in shock as anger was boiling to the surface. His demeanor was so overpowering that Rico felt a sliver of pity for the man that had lived long enough to feel the impending wrath of the CABAL.

Mr. Prescott stood up with the cold composure of a tyrant that had just sentenced his enemies to death. He'd cleared the grief from his continence. He closed his suit jacket, covered up Mikes blood and cleaned his hands on a napkin. He took a long hard look into the eyes of the now shaken street punk. "Actually, let's continue this conversation upstairs. I'd like to show you our suites. Most never get to see them. They're quite breath taking."

Rico could hear police sirens in the distance. The police would be here any moment. Mr. Prescott picked up his phone.

"Yes, do you think you can cover the police? I'm sure there will be questions.Yeah, ok yeah, thank you. I value your help. I've got work to do." then he hung up and spoke to Frxsh and Macktown.

"I'd like a favor. When the police come, tell them the story of how our night got interrupted. After all, you were here. You're just as much of a victim as any of us. My assistant Ramona is coming to speak to the police on my behalf. Follow her lead. I'm sure you'll know what to say. Jelz head upstairs and work on some music. No reason for you to be here for now. I'll call you when things clear up. Mr. Step, please make yourself scarce and let your OG know I'd like to set up a meeting with an S class by Midnight tomorrow. I'd like to know what they know about this. Make that happen, and I'll be sure to tell them the good work you've done tonight. The CABAL owes the AMG a favor because of you. Remember that. Rico, clean up here. Make sure there are no incriminating or personal things floating around, and then quickly meet me upstairs. I'll text you the Suite number. I appreciate all your work, gentlemen."

Rico watched Wiz grab a tablecloth and wrap it around the doomed man's head and lead him to the elevator with Prescott.

Clearing the area didn't take long. Rico gave the police a quick statement and cleared the scene as they began the gristly work of cleaning and investigating what they were now calling a homicide. Adonis had returned assuring Rico that Sienna and her friends were safely taken home. Rico and Adonis headed toward the suite Mr. Prescott had mentioned earlier.

There was little to be said. Rico could see Prescott's eyes were red. He couldn't tell if the large man had shed a tear for a former associate or if it was rage he saw in the eyes of his benefactor. He thought it best to remain silent As they entered the room, Rico could see that it was an incomplete suite.

The floor was made of a rubberized mat and had been completely covered in a tarp. The walls were covered in a carpet like material that had no place on apartment walls. As they moved further into the suite, a door reviled a large room that was empty except that of a table and some chairs as well as a large shower drain. Rico could see Prescott, Wiz and another man with dreadlocks he'd never seen before. The center piece of all the attention was the man captured. He was in his underwear with his legs tied to a backless chair.

Rico could tell the man was in his mid-twenties. There was muscle there and tattoos that looked distinctly like prison tats. His body was covered in bruises and bleeding in some areas. This man was probably feared in some circles. He didn't look like a man confused as to his actions. He had the look of a man that never expected to be at the mercy of those he'd decided to kill. Now here he was on the penthouse floor in an unmarked room that looked like it could have been a public shower or steam room. As Rico surveyed the scene, he noticed that Wiz held an extension cord in his hand. The cord had been branded and was now covered in blood. There were streaks of dried tears on his face, his breathing was labored, and his body was covered in sweat. Rico could tell that Lizard's friend had felt Wiz's fury.

"Rico, Adonis, glad to see you. I wanted to make sure the CABAL was here to welcome our new guest before formally introducing myself. By the way, the man standing next to me is Mr Fox. He's a man that specializes in molding people into whatever I can imagine."

Head nods were silently exchanged. Mr. Prescott then turned toward his prey.

"It's nice to meet you. I'm Ryan Henry Prescott, and this is my establishment. There are so many people that want to be here, apart of ... all this. I've often considered the CABAL to be a sign to the world. That sign is one of hope and prosperity. These grounds are a place where power is built. There is no color or creed. There is only elegance and power...

"It was Liz, man, it wasn't even..." the man began to speak before he was quickly interrupted.

"Mr. Fox, our guest wants to tell us something. Can you help him?"

As if anticipating the command Fox walked over to the man. It was then that Rico noticed that Mr. Fox had on a thin black tool belt. Mr Fox pulled a hammer and box cutter from the belt. After a brief struggle that made Rico nearly lose his stomach, the tip of the man's tongue and most of his teeth had been removed. The man was now a sobbing mess, blood pouring from his mouth.

Without breaking stride, Mr. Prescott continued," as I was saying, The CABAL is a place people work hard to enter. I'm a man that admires hard work. I believe that hard work should be rewarded. The man you have so viciously and senselessly murdered was like a son to me. Mikel was in tune with my philosophies and has been a significant part of my personal and professional growth. He has help make sure this place was a sight to see. If I'm the King of this house Mikel was certainly the prince."

There was a brief pause as Mr. Prescott cleared his throat to regain his composure at the mention of Money Mike.

"I want you to imagine what I saw when I looked at my protege. Better yet, I'd like you to imagine what he saw when he looked at me."

With that, Mr. Prescott and Mr. Fox approached the man. Mr. Fox stood behind the man, now utility knife in hand. Mr. Prescott bent down to look face to face the man.

Speaking in the gravelly voice Rico recognized from earlier that night, Prescott spoke, "I want you to carry the memory of what Mike will never see again."

Rico could only see the back of Mr. Prescott, but he saw Fox grab the man. There were two distinct screams of pain. Mr. Prescott turned and walked to the man's right side. Rico felt a cold sweat as he realized the man's eyes were closed, but blood and a milky fluid were streaming from each of the man's eye sockets. Seeing the calm demeanor of Prescott and the savagery of Mr. Fox made Rico question how this all happened so quickly. He remembered his incident with Lizard the other day with Jelz. He knew they'd roughed Lizard up over a hard drive, but all he gave him was a black eye and bruised ego. Rico couldn't believe that would make the man suicidal enough to attack the CABAL with two people.

Mr. Prescott looked at Rico and Adonis. "Gentlemen, I wanted you to see that your fallen brother will be avenged in a way fitting to his untimely demise. Now I need to figure out why this happened. This was a *senseless* tragedy; therefore, as I extract information from our guest, I'm going to be removing his *senses* as well. This may take a while; you're free to get some rest You'll hear from me soon."

Rico was relieved. He couldn't get out of there fast enough.

twenty-six
slicktalk

THE CABAL HAD BEEN SHUTDOWN for 2 weeks after the death of Money Mike. Mr. Prescott was out of town as usual, and everyone else felt like they'd disappeared from the face of the earth. Adonis had called regularly, but there wasn't much to say until things quieted down. Jelz and Frxsh were working on Frxsh's new album. They'd invited Rico to the studio twice, but he couldn't bring himself to spend much time outside of his place. Rico lived in a crime scene for the second time in his life. He felt like the CABAL would be an escape from this. He could see that he was wrong.

Now, Rico found himself on the longest drive he'd taken in a long time. The police had identified him as a suspect during the night Money Mike was killed. Detectives wanted him to come to answer a few questions about his involvement. Rico knew what to say and what not to say, but the idea that he had been printed and identified as a suspect showed the CABAL was more loyal to its clientele than the clients were to it. Rico decided to take the long route to the police station. They were nice enough to allow him to present himself instead of kicking down the door to his penthouse, so that made him feel a little better...a little. As he drove through Lincoln Way-heading towards the police station. He felt his phone ring. It was Alanna.

" ....Why would you go to the police station without a lawyer. You know the police are dangerous. You're a black man working at an establishment like the CABAL. They're going to try to pin the whole situation on you to make it seem like they've done their jobs!" Alanna seemed more emotional than Rico had seen her lately.

"I live at the CABAL remember? They're hoping I don't come so that they can have a reason to get a warrant and raid the building. I've been there long enough to know better. I'll talk to them. It's not like I killed anybody. Hell, I don't think I even hit anyone. People died. Mr. P and I waited to see who they wanted to talk to. When they said me, he told me I didn't have to go. I told him I'd put us all in danger if I didn't. Mr. P..."

"Damn, man, are you just going to listen to him! Fuck Mr. P and whatever he's talking about. This is YOUR life. You're going to go down for something. How long do you think they've been waiting to take down somebody at the CABAL. That whole place is so fucking shady you're the only person there that feels like they don't belong. You're smart and grounded. Think about it. How many illegal things happen there would happen if you were in charge? Very little, right? That's the problem. You went into a new place with all your talent and skills, and now look, you're caught up in some mess you're not even responsible for ..."

"What if I am responsible?! What if I got Mike killed? I met that nigga Lizard before that night. We had a little scuffle over some property he stole. The nigga wanted some get back. I never expected all this. He went and got his homeboys and decided to crash out. Maybe he was waiting on me. Maybe he was waiting on Jelz."

"Then let Jelz talk to the damn police! You are just so ... you always was just so ..." Alanna paused. Rico thought he could hear her choking back tears. It reminded him of the old days. There was an intense love there, once. It wasn't meant to last, but it was something that was a part of both of them. Rico had almost forgotten. He'd tried so hard to forget about her when she left.

Once she gathered herself, she continued," Please, Rico, why don't you just come here with me. I know some people. You see how I'm able to get around. We can kick it out of state; hell, we can leave the country.

I have money now. I'm not rich, but my life has changed a lot. We don't have to let this happen."

Rico found himself weak at the sound of Alanna's desperation. The flood of emotions was intensified by the stress of the situation. There was love. There was anger. There was sadness.

"See, that's the problem with you. You get into some shit, and then you want to leave. I'm not like that. I face what's coming head-on. I don't abandon people. I don't run."

Silence on the other end. Rico had struck a nerve. Rico knew she'd deserved it after leaving him so suddenly and being gone so long. He knew his words would land hard, but she deserved it. Didn't she?

"Rico, look, I'm sorry. I didn't want to leave like that, but I had to. I wish I could make you understand. I was fighting for so long. I was fighting with you. I was fighting with myself. I had to watch myself fall apart while you were killing yourself to hold me together. I made mistakes, but I'm here now. Things are different. I thought I had more time, but now ... if you weren't involved with these people. I ... I didn't want to come back to town and assume you wanted to see me. I had to pace myself. Then the night we did spend time together, it was even harder. I miss you, and now you're about to put yourself in a position where I can't see you again. So no, maybe it isn't the same, but it's going to feel that way ... for me, it is."

"Look, I'm just going to talk to these people, and I'll meet you later. There's a spot in Rivertown. It's low key. We can talk there."

Rico was uncertain. Apart from him wanting to turn the car around, Alanna was his past. He didn't want to make the same mistakes he'd made before. He wanted to start fresh. He wasn't ready to deal with whatever baggage Alanna had waiting with her. He needed to take his mind off her. He made a call.

"Hello?" Asia answered the phone. "Hi Asia, this is Rico."

The silence before her considered response felt like 5 minutes.

"I didn't think you'd call me, especially after that night."

"If you don't want to talk, that's cool. Just listen. I just feel like I'm about to have a lot going on. I wanted to let you know that the truth is I asked my sister before about you. I just never reached out myself."

"Cause of the Alanna girl, right? Yeah, I know about her. I've been

Sienna's friend for a long time. I knew you all were together; then she left now I heard she's back. Is that what you wanted to tell me?"

"No, I wanted to tell you that ... well ... thank you for the drink. I would like to return the favor soon if you're ever ... well ... thirsty" Rico felt himself fumbling the ball.

"Hmmm ... well, I'd say if you're going to buy me a drink, I want to make sure I'm not sharing my cup with anyone else. I know things can be complicated over time but moving on means not looking back."

"Yeah, you're right about that. I can't even lie. You know it isn't till now I realize we haven't talked that much. I like the way you talk. You sound ... well ... like you got some sense."

Asia laughed,"Well, 2 years at Spellman didn't hurt. Didn't graduate, but the experience helps, I guess. So, I'm assuming you're going to lock my number in cause I'm saving yours. Don't forget you owe me that drink."

"I am, and I won't," Rico said as they exchanged goodbyes.

It was time for Rico to speak to the police. He knew his future was uncertain, but he was willing to face it head-on. The CABAL had been an adventure for him. Now it seemed the adventure was over just as quickly as it started. His questions about his father remained unanswered ... for now

twenty-seven
smallworld

NEARLY TWO WEEKS after the trial, Sienna couldn't help but fear for her Rico's undeserved investigation. Him being the newest face and an apparent target made police all too sure the shooting involved him in some way. Mr. Prescott offered Sienna a position as his assistant to spend some time away from violence, but it wasn't in her to serve in that way. There was nothing left for Sienna but her night work. Mr. P had given her an assignment involving some local Cuban gangsters extorting minority gas station owners for profits and fuel. It wasn't anything special to Sienna, but it would get her mind off things for a while. Fox was setting up her alias and putting her in as a new manager. It'd take a couple of days, but the mousetrap was set, and Sienna needed to sink her teeth into a new mission. She wondered if her desire to become active again resulted from her acclimation to life or if her brother's confinement had given her less to live for. Either way, for her and Cleo, the mission was all that mattered until she received a phone call.

"You have a call from, Bolo. Press 1 to accept"

"What up with you CC?"

"Nothing, just finished a quick workout."

"Tryna keep that ass right, huh," Bolo quipped. Sienna knew he was incorrigible, so she ignored the remark. "Well shit, I found out some.

Remember you asked me about a bit that spilt all the ketchup at that restaurant, and you had to leave?"

Sienna had no idea what Bolo was talking about. It was code, but she had to figure out how to decipher it without giving him away. Ketchup spilled meant blood. A restaurant was a public place. It quickly dawned on her that Bolo had information about her "savior" from her botched Dr. Fowler mission.

"Yeh, I know what you mean; what about it."

"You ever heard of a waitress named something Bradford? A nigga in here came from a rehab spot out in Arizona somewhere crazy like that. He said he was from Rivertown and went to Rehab with the bitch. After rehab, the bitch got picked up in some Fly Lamborghini type shit. Said the bitch was talking to him about learning wet work sum like that. My nigga Rosko told me wet work means a shooter."

Sienna knew exactly what it meant. She wasn't the only one working in town. How many people were out there like her? There was Fox and now this girl. As always, she had more questions than answers.

"Yeah, I've heard of that. Glad she's moved on to bussing tables. Thanks, Bolo."

"Shit Sienna, you straight keep your phone on you; you feel me? Oh yeah, I forgot. Buddy said he didn't know the bit first name, but he knew her nickname."

Sienna's mind was reeling with the information. "What is it?"

"Just some normal shit ... Alanna."

To Be Continued

the cabal: book 2

JANUARY IS the coldest month of the year. The holidays are over for those that can afford the luxury of shit like that. The excitement of a new year isn't felt on the D Pod of the JCF. The First of January is just like any other day. From the facility windows, you can see the snowfall and hear "White Christmas" playing on the radio if you have one. Rico doesn't have any. He's been on a 23-hour lockdown since entering the JCF. He nervously awaited life in General Population. The Guards seemed to Rome the facility looking for people to prey on. They didn't seem human. As far as Rico was concerned, they're animals, plain and simple. They're wild-eyed desperate, and dangerous, but that can be used. Anybody can be used. At least that's the last thing Rico's boy Black told him. But Black was gone. So was Sienna, Prescott, and Jelz. Rico had to embrace his new circumstance for the time being. He knew he couldn't waste his time feeling sorry for himself. Lincoln Way had made him a survivor. Food Shark had made him a hard worker. The CABAL had made him a hustler. That combination for him was Street Knowledge. If confinement is the price of street knowledge, Rico had done his best to stay as ignorant as possible, but now ... now there's just his cell. The people on the outside watch the snowfall, but they don't see it land in the yard turn grey and grimy breakdown into nothing. Ice in the yard is trampled by hordes of lost souls slowly dying in a prison camp not meant to sustain life but to exploit it. People are no different. If you stay in Prison long enough, you become grimy and cold. Life in prison is never-ending winter. No matter how long you try to avoid the cold, eventually, it will find you and freeze you from the inside out. For the JCF, the first sign of winter began with a single snowflake. For Rico, it began when he stepped into the general population. He couldn't help but feel like he'd been here before.

Made in the USA
Monee, IL
12 October 2022

15753204R00094